10-MINUTE BIBLE STORIES FOR TEENS

A MODERN, INTERACTIVE GUIDE TO FOR TODAY'S
YOUTH TO EXPLORE THEIR FAITH, DISCOVER
TIMELESS VALUES, & TACKLE NEW CHALLENGES
WITH GOD'S WISDOM

BIBLICAL TEACHINGS

CONTENTS

AND SO, THE JOURNEY BEGINS...

SCAN ME

Welcome to "*10-Minute Bible Stories for Teens*"! This book is designed specifically for you – a modern teenager trying to figure out life in today's crazy world. Within these pages, you'll find 40 carefully selected Bible stories that will not only deepen your understanding of God's word but also provide you with valuable life lessons and timeless wisdom to help you tackle whatever challenges you face growing up in the 21st century.

We get it – life is busy, and finding time for faith can be tough. That's why each story has been created to take just 10 minutes to read – perfect for those quick breaks between school, sports, and hanging out with friends and family. But don't let the length fool you – they're packed with powerful insights and real-life lessons that will stick with you in your daily life.

How to Use This Book:

1. Take 10 minutes each day to read a story. You can read them in order or pick the one that speaks to you most at any given time. If you want, you can even date each entry to keep track

of your journey. No worries if you miss a day – God's always got your back!

2. Begin by reading the title and the relevant Bible verse to set the context.

3. Next, dive into the story, letting yourself get lost in the narrative and the characters' experiences.

4. Following this, we will connect the story and lessons learned within it to YOU, a modern-day teen, and the problems you might be facing.

5. Now, it's time for the 'Reflection' portion of the story. Take some time to think about your answers to the thought-provoking questions. They'll help you make the story's message a part of your life. You could even write your answers down!

6. End your session with the prayer provided, opening your heart to God and seeking His guidance and strength.

As you explore these stories, you'll encounter epic tales of faith, courage, love, and second chances. From Solomon's wisdom to David's bravery, from Abigail's humility to Jesus' compassion, each story holds valuable lessons that transcend time and speak directly to the heart of modern teenagers like you.

So, get ready to be inspired, challenged, and changed as you discover God's word in a fresh and relevant way. May these stories become a source of comfort, guidance, and motivation as you navigate the thrilling (and sometimes crazy) teenage years. Remember, God's wisdom is timeless, and His love for you never ends.

P.S. Keep your eyes peeled for a possible Part 2 – you never know what God has in store! If you enjoyed this book, don't forget to check out our other books on Amazon.

Old Testament

1

THE STORY OF CREATION

___ / ___ / _____

"For since the creation of the world God's invisible qualities
—his eternal power and divine nature—have been
clearly seen, being understood from what has been
made, so that people are without excuse."

— ROMANS 1:20

In the beginning, God created the heavens and the earth.
The earth was formless and void, and darkness was over
the surface of the deep. The Spirit of God was moving over the
surface of the waters. Over the course of six days, God brought form
and life to the earth. On the first day, He created light and separated it
from the darkness. On the second day, He created the sky and separated the waters above from the waters below. On the third day, God
gathered the waters together and caused dry land to appear, and He
commanded the earth to bring forth vegetation. On the fourth day,
God created the sun, moon, and stars to govern the day and night and
to mark the seasons. On the fifth day, He created the creatures of the
sea and the birds of the air. On the sixth day, God created the land

animals and finally created human beings in His image, male and female.

God formed man from the dust of the ground and breathed life into him, and man became a living being. God placed the man, named Adam, in the Garden of Eden to tend and keep it. God then declared that it was not good for man to be alone, so He caused Adam to fall into a deep sleep. God took one of Adam's ribs and fashioned it into a woman, bringing her to the man. Adam named the woman Eve, as she would become the mother of all the living. God blessed them and commanded them to be fruitful and multiply, and to have dominion over the earth and all its creatures. On the seventh day, God rested from all His work of creation, and He blessed and sanctified the seventh day as a holy day of rest. (Genesis Chapters 1 and 2)

THE STORY OF CREATION, found in the book of Genesis, reveals our Creator's power, wisdom, and love. It also reminds us of the beauty and purpose inherent in all God has made, including ourselves. As teens, it's easy to get caught up in the pressures and challenges of daily life. We might feel insignificant or question our purpose. But the creation story reminds us that we are fearfully and wonderfully made (Psalm 139:14) by a loving God who has a plan for each of us.

Just as God brought order and beauty out of chaos in the beginning, He can bring hope and meaning to our lives, even amid confusion and difficulty. When we take time to appreciate the beauty of God's creation - whether it's a stunning sunset, a majestic mountain, or the laughter of a friend - we are reminded of His love and care for us.

Moreover, as image-bearers of God, we have the unique opportunity to reflect His creativity and love to the world around us. Whether through our talents, our relationships, or our service to others, we can bring beauty and purpose to the lives of those around us, just as God intended from the beginning.

Reflections

• *How can you take time each day to appreciate the beauty of God's creation and remember His love for you?*

• *In what ways can you use your unique talents and abilities to reflect God's creativity and bring beauty to the world around you?*

• *How might understanding your identity as an image-bearer of God change the way you view yourself and others?*

Prayer

Heavenly Father, thank You for the beauty and wonder of Your creation. Help me to see myself and others through Your eyes, recognizing the purpose and potential You have placed within each of us. Give me the strength and wisdom to reflect Your love and creativity in all that I do. Amen.

2

NOAH'S ARK

___ / ___ / _____

"Blessed are all who fear the Lord, who walk in obedience to him."

*G*od saw that the earth was corrupt and filled with violence, so he decided to destroy all living creatures, except for Noah and his family, who found favor in God's eyes. God instructed Noah to build an ark according to specific dimensions and to bring two of every living creature into it, along with his wife, sons, and their wives. Despite the challenges and ridicule he likely faced, Noah did everything God commanded him.

When the flood came, rain fell for forty days and nights, and the waters rose, covering even the highest mountains and destroying all life outside the ark. Noah, his family, and the animals remained safe inside the ark for over a year until the waters receded. After leaving the ark, Noah built an altar and offered sacrifices to God.

God then made a covenant with Noah, promising never again to destroy the earth with a flood. As a sign of this covenant, God set a

4

rainbow in the sky. The story of Noah and the ark demonstrates faith, obedience, and God's mercy, showing that God provides salvation for those who trust in Him and walk according to His commands, even in the face of overwhelming wickedness.

As TEENS, you face countless decisions and pressures every day. It can be tempting to follow the crowd or to make choices based on what seems easiest or most popular. However, Noah's story reminds us that true fulfillment and purpose come from obeying God, even when it's challenging.

When you choose to obey God's commands and follow his will for your life, you align yourself with his perfect plan and open yourself to his blessings. This may mean making difficult choices, such as standing up for what's right, even when others don't understand or support you. It may involve stepping out in faith and trusting God to guide you through unknown territory.

Remember, obedience to God is not about earning his love or salvation, which are already freely given through Jesus Christ. Instead, it's a response to his love and a desire to grow closer to him. By obeying God, you demonstrate your trust in his wisdom and goodness, and you allow him to work in and through your life in powerful ways.

Reflection

• *What are some areas of your life where you struggle to obey God? How can you lean on his strength and grace to help you make choices that honor him?*

• *Think about a time when you obeyed God, even when it was difficult. How did that experience shape your faith and your understanding of God's character?*

• *In what ways can you encourage and support your friends to obey God, even when they face pressure to conform to the world's standards?*

Prayer

Dear God, thank you for the example of Noah and his obedience to you. Help me to trust in your wisdom and to follow your will for my life, even when it's challenging. Give me the courage to stand for what's right and to lead others closer to you through my obedience. Amen.

3

THE CURSE OF HAM

___ / ___ / _____

"Honor your father and your mother, so that you may live
long in the land the Lord your God is giving you."

— EXODUS 20:12

After the flood, Noah, a man of the soil, began to cultivate the land and planted a vineyard. As an experienced farmer, Noah likely used his knowledge and skills to grow grapes and produce wine. One day, he drank some of the wine from his vineyard and became drunk, lying uncovered in his tent. This incident highlights Noah's human frailty and the potential dangers of excessive alcohol consumption.

Ham, the father of Canaan and one of Noah's three sons, saw his father's nakedness and told his two brothers outside. Instead of respectfully covering his father, Ham chose to share what he had seen with his siblings. This action was seen as disrespectful and a violation of Noah's privacy and dignity.

In contrast, Shem and Japheth, the other two sons, responded with reverence and discretion. They took a garment and laid it across their shoulders, walking backward into the tent to cover their father's naked body. They kept their faces turned away to avoid seeing their father's nakedness, demonstrating their respect and desire to protect Noah's honor.

When Noah awoke from his drunken state, he learned what his youngest son, Ham, had done to him. In response, Noah pronounced a curse, saying, "Cursed be Canaan; a servant of servants shall he be to his brothers." This curse was directed at Canaan, Ham's son, and his descendants. It suggests that Ham's disrespectful actions would have consequences that would impact his lineage.

Noah then blessed Shem and Japheth for their honorable conduct. He declared, "Blessed be the Lord, the God of Shem; and let Canaan be his servant." This blessing acknowledged Shem's righteousness and his relationship with God, while also reaffirming the curse on Canaan as a servant to Shem. Additionally, Noah blessed Japheth, saying, "May God enlarge Japheth, and let him dwell in the tents of Shem, and let Canaan be his servant." This blessing indicated that Japheth's descendants would prosper and have a close relationship with Shem's lineage, while Canaan would remain subservient to both.

The story of Noah's drunkenness and his sons' actions emphasizes the importance of respect, honor, and the far-reaching consequences of choices, setting the stage for the development of the Israelite nation through Shem's line and the subjugation of the Canaanites, descendants of Ham. This narrative highlights the significance of family dynamics, the transmission of blessings and curses, and the long-term impact of individual actions in the biblical context.

THE STORY of Noah and his sons, found in the book of Genesis, teaches us important lessons about respecting our parents and elders.

After the great flood, Noah's sons faced a choice in how they would treat their father during a vulnerable moment, and their actions had lasting consequences.

It's not always easy to honor and respect our parents and elders, especially when we disagree with them or feel like they don't understand us. However, the story of Noah and his sons reminds us that the way we treat our parents and elders matters to God and can have far-reaching consequences in our lives.

Shem and Japheth demonstrated respect for their father by covering his nakedness and protecting his dignity, even in a challenging situation. As a result, they received a blessing from their father. In contrast, Ham's disrespectful behavior led to negative consequences for his descendants.

In our own lives, we can show honor to our parents and elders by speaking to them respectfully, even when we disagree, and by looking for ways to serve and support them. This might mean helping out with chores at home, offering to run errands, or simply taking the time to listen and express appreciation for their guidance and care. By choosing to honor our parents and elders, we not only obey God's command (Ephesians 6:1-3) but also develop character qualities like humility, compassion, and selflessness that will serve us well in all our relationships.

Reflection

• *In what practical ways can you show honor and respect to your parents and elders, even when it's challenging?*

• *How might choosing to honor your parents and elders impact your other relationships and your personal growth?*

• *In what areas of your life do you need God's help to develop a more respectful and honoring attitude toward authority figures?*

Prayer

HEAVENLY FATHER, thank You for the parents and elders You have placed in my life. Help me to honor and respect them, even in difficult moments. Amen.

4

ABRAM'S JOURNEY TO CANAAN

___ / ___ / _____

"For I know the plans I have for you," declares the Lord,
"plans to prosper you and not to harm you, plans to give
you hope and a future."

— JEREMIAH 29:11

God called Abram to leave his homeland of Haran and go to a land that He would show him. God promised to make Abram into a great nation, to bless him, to make his name great, and to bless all the peoples of the earth through him. Abram, at the age of 75, obeyed God's call and set out with his wife Sarai, his nephew Lot, and all their possessions.

They journeyed to the land of Canaan, and upon arriving, God appeared to Abram and said, "To your offspring I will give this land." Abram built an altar there to the Lord. As they continued their journey, Abram built altars and called on the name of the Lord at various locations, including Bethel and Ai.

However, a famine struck the land of Canaan, and Abram decided to go down to Egypt to escape the harsh conditions. As they approached

Egypt, Abram told his wife Sarai to say that she was his sister, fearing that the Egyptians would kill him and take her because of her beauty. When they entered Egypt, Sarai's beauty was indeed noticed, and she was taken into Pharaoh's palace. God afflicted Pharaoh and his household with great plagues because of Sarai. Pharaoh, realizing the truth, confronted Abram and sent him away with his wife and all his possessions. (Genesis Chapter 12)

THE STORY of Abraham and Sarah, found in the book of Genesis, is a powerful example of trusting in God's plan even when it seems impossible. Despite facing many challenges and setbacks, Abraham and Sarah held onto their faith in God's promise to bless them with a child and make them into a great nation.

When we're young, it can be easy to feel like our lives are not going according to plan. We may face disappointments, obstacles, or unfulfilled dreams that leave us questioning God's purpose for our lives. However, the story of Abraham and Sarah reminds us that God's plans are often beyond our understanding and may require us to trust Him even when the path ahead seems uncertain.

Like Abraham and Sarah, we may face setbacks or periods of waiting that test our faith. However, we can choose to hold onto God's promises and trust that He is working behind the scenes to bring about His good purposes in our lives. This might mean continuing to pray and seek God's guidance even when we don't see immediate answers or stepping out in faith to follow God's leading even when it takes us outside of our comfort zones.

As we trust in God's plan, we can find peace and purpose even in the midst of life's challenges. We can also be encouraged by the knowledge that God desires to bless us and use our lives to impact others, just as He blessed Abraham and Sarah and used their story to bless all the peoples of the earth.

Reflection

• *In what areas of your life do you need to trust God's plan more fully, even if you can't see the outcome yet?*

• *How can you cultivate a deeper trust in God's promises and purposes for your life, even in the face of setbacks or disappointments?*

• *What steps can you take to seek God's guidance and direction as you navigate the challenges and decisions of teenage life?*

Prayer

Heavenly Father, thank You for the example of Abraham and Sarah, who trusted in Your plan even when the path ahead was uncertain. Help me to trust You more deeply with every aspect of my life, knowing that You are working all things together for my good and Your glory. Amen.

5

JOSEPH AND HIS BROTHERS

___ / ___ / _____

"Get rid of all bitterness, rage and anger, brawling and slander, along with every form of malice. Be kind and compassionate to one another, forgiving each other, just as in Christ God forgave you."

— EPHESIANS 4:31-32

*J*oseph, the eleventh son of Jacob (also known as Israel), was his father's favorite child. This favoritism, along with Joseph's dreams of his brothers bowing down to him, caused his brothers to resent him. One day, while Joseph was checking on his brothers as they were tending their father's flocks, the brothers seized him, stripped him of his special robe, and threw him into a pit. They then sold him into slavery to a group of Ishmaelite traders headed for Egypt.

In Egypt, Joseph was bought by Potiphar, an officer of Pharaoh, and became successful in his household. However, Potiphar's wife falsely accused Joseph of attempting to sleep with her, and he was thrown into prison. While in prison, Joseph interpreted the dreams of two of

Pharaoh's servants, the cupbearer and the baker. His interpretations came true, but the cupbearer forgot about Joseph after he was restored to his position.

Two years later, Pharaoh had a dream that no one could interpret. The cupbearer remembered Joseph and told Pharaoh about him. Joseph was brought before Pharaoh and interpreted the dream, predicting seven years of abundance followed by seven years of famine. Impressed by Joseph's wisdom, Pharaoh appointed him as second-in-command over Egypt and put him in charge of preparing for the famine.

During the famine, Joseph's brothers came to Egypt to buy grain, not recognizing Joseph as the brother they had sold into slavery. After testing their character, Joseph eventually revealed his identity and forgave his brothers, recognizing that God had sent him ahead to preserve their lives and the lives of many others. Joseph's family, including his father Jacob, moved to Egypt and settled in the land of Goshen. (Genesis Chapters 37-50)

THE STORY of Joseph and his brothers, found in the book of Genesis, is a remarkable example of the power of forgiveness. Despite facing betrayal, injustice, and hardship, Joseph chose to forgive his brothers and trust in God's plan for his life, ultimately leading to reconciliation and blessing for his entire family.

Throughout life, we may face hurt, betrayal, or mistreatment from others, whether it's a family member, friend, or classmate. In these moments, it can be tempting to hold onto anger, bitterness, or a desire for revenge. However, Joseph's story reminds us of the transformative power of forgiveness.

Forgiveness doesn't mean excusing or forgetting the wrong that was done to us. Rather, it means choosing to release our grip on anger and resentment and trusting God to bring healing and justice in His way and time. As we forgive others, we open the door for reconciliation, peace, and freedom in our hearts and relationships. Moreover, extending forgiveness can be a powerful witness to others of God's love and grace. When we choose to forgive, we reflect the mercy and compassion that God has shown to us through Christ, who died on the cross to forgive our sins and reconcile us to Himself.

Reflection

• *Is there someone in your life whom you need to forgive? What steps can you take to begin the process of forgiveness, even if the other person hasn't apologized or changed their behavior?*

• *How might choosing to forgive others impact your own emotional and spiritual well-being, as well as your relationships with others?*

• *In what ways can you trust God to bring justice and healing in situations where you have been wronged, even as you seek to forgive and release bitterness?*

Prayer

Heavenly Father, thank You for the example of Joseph, who chose to forgive his brothers even after enduring great hardship and injustice. Help me to extend that same forgiveness to others, trusting in Your power to bring healing, reconciliation, and redemption in my life and relationships. Amen.

6

JOSEPH AND POTIPHAR'S WIFE

___ / ___ / _____

"No temptation has overtaken you except what is common to mankind. And God is faithful; he will not let you be tempted beyond what you can bear. But when you are tempted, he will also provide a way out so that you can endure it."

— 1 CORINTHIANS 10:13

*A*fter being sold into slavery by his brothers, Joseph was bought by Potiphar, an officer of Pharaoh and the captain of the guard in Egypt. The Lord was with Joseph, and he became successful in Potiphar's household. Potiphar recognized that God was with Joseph and that He made everything Joseph did prosper. As a result, Potiphar put Joseph in charge of his entire household and entrusted him with all his possessions.

Joseph was well-built and handsome, and after some time, Potiphar's wife took notice of him. She repeatedly tried to seduce Joseph, saying, "Lie with me." However, Joseph refused her advances, stating that he could not betray his master's trust or sin against God.

Despite her persistent attempts, Joseph continued to refuse her day after day.

One day, when Joseph went into the house to attend to his duties, none of the household servants were inside. Potiphar's wife caught him by his garment, saying, "Lie with me." Joseph left his garment in her hand and fled from the house. Angry and humiliated, Potiphar's wife called for the household servants and accused Joseph of trying to sleep with her, using the garment as evidence. When Potiphar heard his wife's story, he became furious and had Joseph thrown into prison.

However, even in prison, the Lord was with Joseph and showed him steadfast love. The keeper of the prison put Joseph in charge of all the prisoners, and whatever he did, the Lord made it succeed. (Genesis Chapter 39)

THE STORY of Joseph and Potiphar's wife, found in the book of Genesis, is a powerful example of maintaining integrity and trusting God in the face of temptation and false accusations. Despite facing pressure to compromise his values, Joseph chose to honor God and flee from sexual immorality.

As teenagers, we face many temptations and pressures to compromise our values and faith. Whether it's pressure to engage in sexual activity, cheat in school, or participate in bullying or gossip, it can be challenging to stand firm in our convictions. However, Joseph's story reminds us of the importance of maintaining our integrity and trusting God, even when doing the right thing comes at a cost.

Like Joseph, we may face false accusations or negative consequences for choosing to honor God and follow His standards. However, we can trust that God is with us and will ultimately work all things together for our good and His glory. Moreover, by choosing to flee from temptation and live with integrity, we protect ourselves from the harmful consequences of sin and maintain a clear conscience before God and others. This doesn't mean we will never make mistakes, but it does mean that we can seek God's strength and grace to help us make wise choices and honor Him in every area of our lives.

Reflection

• *In what areas of your life are you currently facing temptation or pressure to compromise your values? What practical steps can you take to resist temptation and maintain your integrity?*

• *How can you trust God and lean on His strength when you face false accusations or negative consequences for doing the right thing?*

• *In what ways can living a life of integrity and purity impact your witness to others and bring glory to God?*

Prayer

Heavenly Father, thank You for the example of Joseph, who maintained his integrity and trust in You even in the face of temptation and false accusations. Give me the strength to resist temptation, flee from sin, and honor You in every area of my life. May my choices bring glory to Your name. Amen.

7

THE TABERNACLE CRAFTSMEN

___ / ___ / _____

"Now to each one the manifestation of the Spirit is given for
the common good."

— 1 CORINTHIANS 12:7

*A*fter giving Moses the Ten Commandments and instructions for building the Tabernacle, God appointed Bezalel from the tribe of Judah and Oholiab from the tribe of Dan to oversee the construction of the Tabernacle and its furnishings. God filled them with His Spirit, giving them wisdom, understanding, knowledge, and skill in all kinds of craftsmanship.

Bezalel was skilled in working with gold, silver, bronze, stone cutting, and wood carving. He was also an expert in designing artistic works. Oholiab was skilled in engraving, designing, and embroidering using blue, purple, and scarlet yarn and fine linen.

God gave these two men the ability to teach others, and they were put in charge of all the skilled workers who would construct the Tabernacle and its furnishings according to the instructions given to Moses. They were responsible for overseeing the construction of the

Ark of the Covenant, the Table of Showbread, the Lampstand, the Altar of Incense, the Altar of Burnt Offering, and the Basin for washing, as well as the garments for the priests.

Bezalel, Oholiab, and their skilled team worked diligently to create all the items needed for the Tabernacle, using the materials donated by the Israelites. They followed God's instructions precisely, ensuring that everything was made according to the pattern shown to Moses on the mountain. (Exodus Chapters 31, and 35 to 39)

THE STORY of Bezalel and Oholiab, found in the book of Exodus, demonstrates how God uniquely gifts individuals with specific talents and abilities to accomplish His purposes. As we explore their story, we'll discover the importance of recognizing and using our own God-given talents to serve others and honor God.

At different times throughout your life (especially your teens), you may be find yourself in a season of discovering and developing your own unique talents and abilities. Like Bezalel and Oholiab, each of you has been created by God with specific gifts and passions that can be used to serve others and bring glory to Him.

Your talents may lie in areas such as music, art, writing, athletics, technology, or leadership. Or perhaps you have a heart for compassion and serving others. Whatever your unique gifts may be, they are not an accident or coincidence - they are a part of God's intentional design for your life.

As you seek to discover and cultivate your talents, remember that they are ultimately given to you by God to be used for His purposes. This means using your gifts not just for personal gain or recognition, but to bless others, build up the church, and point people to Christ.

Just as Bezalel and Oholiab used their artistic abilities to create a beautiful space for God's presence to dwell, you too can use your talents to create a space for God to work in the lives of those around you.

Reflection

• *What talents or abilities has God given you? How can you use these gifts to serve others and honor God?*

• *Are there any talents you have been hesitant to use or develop? What steps can you take to overcome fear or insecurity and step out in faith to use these gifts?*

• *How can you cultivate a heart of humility and gratitude as you use your talents, recognizing that they are ultimately a gift from God to be used for His glory?*

Prayer

Heavenly Father, thank You for the unique talents and abilities You have given me. Help me to discover and develop these gifts, using them to serve others and bring glory to Your name. May I steward these talents with humility and gratitude, knowing that they are a reflection of Your creative design. Amen.

8

THE FIERY FURNACE

___ / ___ / _____

"Do not be conformed to this world, but be transformed by the renewal of your mind, that by testing you may discern what is the will of God, what is good and acceptable and perfect."

— ROMANS 12:2

*D*uring the reign of King Jehoiakim of Judah, Nebuchadnezzar, king of Babylon, besieged Jerusalem and took many of the Israelites captive, including Daniel, Hananiah, Mishael, and Azariah. These four young men were chosen to serve in Nebuchadnezzar's court and were given new names: Belteshazzar (Daniel), Shadrach (Hananiah), Meshach (Mishael), and Abednego (Azariah).

Despite being in a foreign land, the four young men remained faithful to God and refused to defile themselves by eating the king's food and wine. They requested permission to eat only vegetables and drink water, and God blessed them with knowledge, skill, and wisdom. When the king tested them, he found them ten times better than all the magicians and enchanters in his kingdom.

Later, King Nebuchadnezzar created a giant golden statue and commanded everyone to bow down and worship it whenever they heard the sound of musical instruments. Shadrach, Meshach, and Abednego refused to worship the idol, staying true to their faith in God. Furious, the king ordered them to be thrown into a fiery furnace, heated seven times hotter than usual.

However, when the king looked into the furnace, he saw four men walking unharmed in the midst of the flames, and the fourth looked like a divine being. Nebuchadnezzar called the three men out of the furnace and praised their God, who had sent His angel to deliver them. The king then promoted Shadrach, Meshach, and Abednego to higher positions in the province of Babylon. (Daniel Chapters 1 and 3)

THE STORY of Daniel and his friends, Shadrach, Meshach, and Abednego, found in the book of Daniel, is a powerful example of standing firm in one's beliefs despite intense peer pressure. As we explore their story, we'll discover the importance of staying true to our faith and values, even when it's difficult or unpopular.

As teenagers, you likely face daily pressure to conform to the world's standards and expectations. Whether it's pressure to engage in risky behaviors, compromise your beliefs, or simply fit in with the crowd, standing firm in your faith can be challenging.

However, Daniel and his friends remind us that we don't have to give in to peer pressure or compromise our values to be accepted or successful. Instead, we can choose to honor God and trust Him to guide and protect us, even in difficult circumstances.

This doesn't mean that standing up for your beliefs will always be easy or popular. You may face ridicule, rejection, or even persecution for choosing to follow God's ways rather than the world's. But like Shadrach, Meshach, and Abednego, you can trust that God is with you in the fire and will ultimately use your faithfulness for His glory and your good.

As you navigate the pressures and challenges of teenage life, remember that your identity and worth are found in Christ, not in the approval of others. Surround yourself with friends and mentors who will encourage you in your faith, and don't be afraid to be a positive influence and example to those around you.

Reflection

• *In what areas of your life do you feel the most pressure to conform to the world's standards? How can you stand firm in your faith and values in these situations?*

• *Who are some trusted friends or mentors you can turn to for support and encouragement when you face peer pressure or difficult decisions?*

• *How can you use your influence and example to positively impact others and point them to Christ, even in the face of opposition or pressure to conform?*

Prayer

Heavenly Father, thank You for the courage and faithfulness of Daniel, Shadrach, Meshach, and Abednego. Give me the strength to stand firm in my beliefs, even when it's difficult or unpopular. Help me to find my identity and worth in You, and to be a positive influence for Your kingdom. Amen.

9

THE LION'S DEN

___ / ___ / _____

"Have I not commanded you? Be strong and courageous. Do
not be afraid; do not be discouraged, for the Lord your
God will be with you wherever you go."

— JOSHUA 1:9

*D*aniel, a young Jewish man serving in the court of King
Darius, faced a severe test of his faith when his enemies
devised a plan to trap him. They convinced the king to issue a decree
forbidding anyone from praying to any god or man except the king
for thirty days, with the penalty of being thrown into a den of lions.
Despite the dire consequences, Daniel refused to compromise his
faith and continued to pray to God three times a day, just as he had
always done.

When Daniel's enemies caught him in the act of prayer and reported
him to the king, Darius was distressed, realizing he had been manip-
ulated. However, the law could not be altered, and the king was
forced to abide by his own edict. With a heavy heart, King Darius

ordered Daniel to be cast into the den of lions, hoping that Daniel's God would deliver him.

Throughout the night, the king fasted and anxiously waited for morning. At dawn, he rushed to the lions' den and called out to Daniel, who replied that God had sent His angel to protect him from harm. Overjoyed, King Darius ordered Daniel to be removed from the den and decreed that all people in his kingdom should fear and reverence the God of Daniel.

This story showcases Daniel's unwavering faith, courage, and commitment to God, even in the face of great personal risk. It demonstrates the power of prayer, the faithfulness of God to protect and deliver those who trust in Him, and the impact that one person's faith can have on others.

You'll likely face situations where your beliefs and values are challenged or where you feel pressure to compromise your faith. Daniel's story reminds us that it takes courage to stand firm in what you believe, especially when the consequences may be difficult or unpopular.

When you choose to stand for your beliefs, you demonstrate the depth of your faith and your commitment to following God, no matter the cost. This may mean facing criticism, ridicule, or even persecution from others who don't share your values. However, just as God protected and vindicated Daniel, he will also be with you as you stand for what is right.

Remember, your courage to stand for your beliefs can have a powerful impact on those around you. By remaining steadfast in your faith, you serve as a light in a world that often seems dark and confusing. Your example can inspire others to seek truth and to live with integrity, even in the face of challenges.

Reflection

• *What are some of your core beliefs and values? How can you cultivate the courage to stand for these beliefs, even when it's difficult?*

• *Think about a time when you faced pressure to compromise your faith or values. How did you respond, and what did you learn from that experience?*

• *In what ways can you support and encourage your friends and peers who are also striving to stand for their beliefs?*

Prayer

Dear God, thank you for the example of Daniel and his courage to stand for his faith. Give me the strength and boldness to remain true to my beliefs, even in the face of adversity. May my life be a testimony to your goodness and a light to those around me. Amen.

JONAH AND THE WHALE

___ / ___ / _____

"Consider it pure joy, my brothers and sisters, whenever
you face trials of many kinds, because you know that
the testing of your faith produces perseverance. Let
perseverance finish its work so that you may be mature
and complete, not lacking anything."

— JAMES 1:2-4

God called Jonah, a prophet, to go to the city of Nineveh and preach against its wickedness. However, Jonah disobeyed God and attempted to flee from His presence by boarding a ship bound for Tarshish. During the journey, a severe storm arose, and the sailors cast lots to determine who was responsible for the calamity. The lot fell on Jonah, and he confessed to fleeing from God. Jonah told the sailors to throw him overboard to calm the sea, and they reluctantly did so.

As Jonah sank into the depths, God appointed a great fish to swallow him. Jonah remained in the belly of the fish for three days and three nights. While inside the fish, Jonah prayed to God, acknowledging his disobedience and praising God for His mercy. God then commanded the fish, and it vomited Jonah onto dry land.

After this, God called Jonah a second time to go to Nineveh and preach His message. This time, Jonah obeyed and went to the city, proclaiming that in forty days, Nineveh would be overthrown. The people of Nineveh, from the king to the lowest citizen, believed Jonah's message and repented, proclaiming a fast and putting on sackcloth. When God saw their repentance, He relented from the disaster He had threatened to bring upon the city.

Jonah, however, grew angry because God spared Nineveh. He went outside the city and made a shelter, waiting to see what would happen. God appointed a plant to provide shade for Jonah, but then sent a worm to damage the plant, causing it to wither. As the sun beat down on Jonah, he grew faint and wished to die. God used this situation to teach Jonah a lesson about His compassion and mercy, even for those whom Jonah considered undeserving. (Jonah)

THE STORY of Jonah and the Whale, found in the book of Jonah, teaches us valuable lessons about the consequences of disobedience and the importance of learning from our mistakes. As we explore Jonah's journey, we'll discover how God's mercy and grace can transform even our greatest failures into opportunities for growth and redemption.

It's important to remember that we all make mistakes - no matter how perfect a person may seem. Whether it's disobeying our parents, hurting a friend's feelings, or making poor choices, we can often find ourselves facing the consequences of our actions. However, Jonah's story reminds us that our mistakes don't have to define us and that God's mercy and grace are always available to us when we turn to Him in repentance.

Like Jonah, we may sometimes try to run from God's plan for our lives or ignore His guidance. But as we see in the story, disobedience only leads to chaos and heartache. When we make mistakes, it's essential to take responsibility for our actions, seek forgiveness, and learn from the experience.

God's discipline, as seen in Jonah's time in the belly of the fish, is not meant to punish us but to guide us back to the right path. When we humble ourselves and turn to God, He is faithful to forgive us and provide a way forward.

Moreover, our mistakes and failures can often become powerful testimonies of God's transformative work in our lives. Just as Jonah's disobedience ultimately led to the repentance of an entire city, God can use our stories of redemption to impact others and point them to His love and grace.

Reflection

• *Reflect on a time when you made a mistake or disobeyed God. What consequences did you face, and what lessons did you learn from the experience?*

• *How can you cultivate a heart of repentance and humility when you make mistakes, instead of running from God or trying to hide your failures?*

• *In what ways can your story of God's mercy and redemption in your life be used to encourage others and point them to Christ?*

Prayer

Heavenly Father, thank You for the story of Jonah, which reminds us of Your endless mercy and grace. When I make mistakes, help me to turn to You in repentance, learning from my failures and trusting in Your power to redeem and restore. May my story be a testament to Your transformative love. Amen.

THE STORY OF RUTH

___ / ___ / _____

*"Two are better than one, because they have a good reward
for their toil. For if they fall, one will lift up his fellow.
But woe to him who is alone when he falls and has not
another to lift him up!"*

— ECCLESIASTES 4:9-10

In a time of famine, Naomi, her husband, and their two
sons fled Bethlehem for the land of Moab. Tragedy struck
when Naomi's husband and sons died, leaving her and her daugh-
ters-in-law, Orpah and Ruth, as widows in a foreign land. Naomi,
heartbroken, decided to return to her homeland. Orpah reluctantly
returned to her own family, but Ruth clung to Naomi, vowing to stay
with her and embrace her God and people.

Upon arriving in Bethlehem during the barley harvest, Ruth gleaned
grain in the fields of Boaz, a relative of Naomi's late husband. Boaz,
moved by Ruth's devotion and hard work, ensured she was treated
well. Following Naomi's instruction, Ruth sought Boaz's protection as

a kinsman-redeemer. Boaz agreed to marry Ruth after a closer relative declined.

Their marriage was blessed with a son, Obed, who became the grandfather of King David. Ruth's unwavering loyalty to Naomi and Boaz's kindness exemplify hesed - the steadfast love and covenant loyalty that goes beyond expectation. The Book of Ruth demonstrates how God works through human acts of faithfulness to preserve Naomi's family line and provide a future for His people, weaving even the most unlikely of stories into His greater plan.

IN THE STORY of Ruth and Naomi, found in the book of Ruth, we find a beautiful story of friendship between two women, Ruth and Naomi, that teaches us the value of loyalty, selflessness, and unwavering support.

As teens, you understand the importance of friendship in your lives. Friends are the people who stand by you through thick and thin, celebrate your successes, and comfort you in times of sorrow. The story of Ruth and Naomi exemplifies the power of true friendship and the blessings that come from putting others first.

Just like Ruth, you may face difficult decisions that test your loyalty to your friends. You might be tempted to prioritize your own interests or follow the crowd, even if it means leaving a friend behind. However, Ruth's example encourages us to be steadfast in our friendships, even when it's challenging.

Moreover, Ruth's story teaches us that genuine friendship involves selflessness and a willingness to serve. By working hard to provide for Naomi, Ruth demonstrated her love and commitment to their friendship. As teens, you can show your friends the same kind of dedication by being there for them during tough times, offering a listening ear, or lending a helping hand.

Remember, the friendships you cultivate now can have a lasting impact on your life and the lives of those around you. By embodying the qualities of loyalty, selflessness, and unwavering support, you can build friendships that will not only enrich your teenage years but also lay the foundation for meaningful relationships in adulthood.

Reflection

• *How can you demonstrate loyalty and unwavering support to your friends, even when it's difficult?*

• *In what ways can you serve your friends and put their needs before your own?*

• *How might your friendships inspire others and point them toward a deeper relationship with God?*

Prayer

Dear God, thank You for the gift of friendship and the example of Ruth and Naomi. Help us to be loyal, selfless, and supportive friends, just as Ruth was to Naomi. Give us the courage to stand by our friends through life's challenges and the wisdom to cultivate friendships that honor You. Amen.

12

THE RISE AND FALL OF KING SOLOMON

___ / ___ / _____

*"Let the wise hear and increase in learning, and the one
who understands obtain guidance."*

— PROVERBS 1:5

*S*olomon, the son of King David and Bathsheba, ascended to
the throne of Israel after his father's death. He prayed to
God for wisdom to govern his people, and God granted him unparalleled wisdom along with great riches and honor. Solomon's wisdom
was famously put to the test when two women came to him, both
claiming to be the mother of the same baby. Solomon's clever solution was to suggest cutting the baby in half, revealing the true mother
as the one willing to give up her child to save its life.

As king, Solomon undertook ambitious building projects, including
the magnificent Temple in Jerusalem, which would serve as the
center of Israelite worship, and a grand palace for himself. He formed
strategic alliances with neighboring kingdoms and engaged in extensive trade, bringing unprecedented wealth and prosperity to Israel.
However, despite his wisdom, Solomon was not immune to human

weaknesses. He took many foreign wives, who influenced him to worship their gods, turning his heart away from the Lord. This angered God, who had commanded the Israelites to worship Him alone. As a consequence, God declared that the kingdom would be divided after Solomon's death, with only one tribe remaining loyal to Solomon's descendants.

Solomon reigned over Israel for 40 years, a period marked by peace, prosperity, and cultural flourishing. He composed thousands of proverbs and songs, and his wisdom attracted visitors from far and wide, including the Queen of Sheba. However, his legacy was tarnished by his disobedience to God and his failure to lead the people in faithful worship. After Solomon's death, his son Rehoboam took the throne, but his harsh policies led to the division of the kingdom. The ten northern tribes rebelled and formed the Kingdom of Israel, while Rehoboam retained control over the southern Kingdom of Judah. This division marked the beginning of a tumultuous period in Israelite history and set the stage for the eventual downfall and exile of both kingdoms.

IN THE STORY OF SOLOMON, found in the book of 1 Kings, we discover the incredible story of King Solomon, who, when given the opportunity to ask for anything from God, chose to request wisdom above all else.

Right now, you're at a stage in your life where you're making decisions that could shape your future. Like Solomon, you have the opportunity to prioritize learning and seeking wisdom above all else. Solomon's story teaches us that true wisdom comes from God and that when we earnestly seek it, God is more than willing to grant it to us.

In today's world, it's easy to get caught up in the pursuit of temporary things like popularity, material possessions, or success. However, Solomon's example reminds us that the most valuable thing we can strive for is wisdom. By making learning a lifelong pursuit, you can gain the knowledge and understanding needed to navigate life's challenges, make wise decisions, and positively impact those around you.

Moreover, seeking wisdom is not just about academic knowledge; it's about growing in your understanding of God and His ways. As you study the Bible, pray, and surround yourself with wise mentors, you'll develop a deeper relationship with God and gain invaluable insights for living a life that honors Him.

Remember, just as God was pleased with Solomon's request for wisdom, He delights in seeing you pursue wisdom and understanding. Embrace the value of lifelong learning, and trust that God will guide you every step of the way.

Reflection

• *In what areas of your life do you need to seek wisdom from God?*

• *How can you prioritize learning and growing in your relationship with God amidst the distractions of daily life?*

• *What practical steps can you take to surround yourself with wise mentors and resources that will help you grow in wisdom?*

Prayer

Dear God, thank You for the example of Solomon and the value of seeking wisdom. Help us to prioritize learning and growing in our understanding of You and Your ways. Grant us the wisdom we need to navigate life's challenges and make decisions that honor You. May we never stop pursuing wisdom and knowledge all the days of our lives. Amen.

13

THE STORY OF SAMSON

___ / ___ / _____

*"Like a city whose walls are broken through is a person who
lacks self-control."*

— PROVERBS 25:28

*S*amson, a man chosen by God to deliver Israel from the
oppression of the Philistines, was born to a couple who had
been unable to conceive. An angel of the Lord appeared to Samson's
mother, announcing that she would bear a son who would be a
Nazirite, dedicated to God from birth. As a Nazirite, Samson was to
abstain from wine, avoid contact with the dead, and never cut his
hair. As Samson grew, God blessed him with incredible strength,
which he used to fight against the Philistines, performing feats such
as killing a lion with his bare hands and defeating a thousand men
with only the jawbone of a donkey.

Despite his God-given strength and purpose, Samson struggled with
self-control, particularly when it came to women. He married a
Philistine woman, going against God's command not to intermarry

with the pagan nations. Later, he fell in love with a woman named Delilah, who was secretly working with the Philistine leaders to discover the source of Samson's strength. After several attempts, Samson finally revealed that his strength came from his uncut hair, a symbol of his dedication to God as a Nazirite. While Samson slept, Delilah cut his hair, rendering him powerless. The Philistines captured him, gouged out his eyes, and forced him to work as a slave in their temple.

In captivity, Samson's hair began to grow back, and he called out to God, asking for strength one last time. During a Philistine celebration in the temple of their god Dagon, Samson was brought out to entertain the crowd. Seizing the opportunity, Samson prayed to God, and God granted him the strength to push against the pillars of the temple, causing it to collapse. In this final act, Samson killed himself along with many Philistines, fulfilling his purpose as a deliverer of Israel. Samson's story serves as a cautionary tale, demonstrating the importance of obedience to God and the consequences of allowing one's weaknesses to overshadow one's God-given purpose. It also highlights God's power to use imperfect individuals to accomplish His will and deliver His people from oppression.

IN THE STORY of Samson found in the book of Judges, we find the story of Samson, a man chosen by God to deliver Israel from the Philistines. Samson's life serves as a powerful reminder of the importance of self-control and the consequences of giving in to temptation.

How often do you face numerous temptations and distractions? They can easily pull you away from God's plan for your life. Like Samson, you may find yourself drawn to things that seem appealing but ultimately lead to negative consequences.

One of the key lessons from Samson's life is the importance of guarding your heart and mind. Proverbs 4:23 tells us, "Above all else, guard your heart, for everything you do flows from it." When you allow temptation to take root in your thoughts and desires, it becomes increasingly difficult to resist. This can lead to poor choices, damaged relationships, and a weakened relationship with God.

However, the good news is that God provides a way out of temptation. 1 Corinthians 10:13 says, "No temptation has overtaken you except what is common to mankind. And God is faithful; he will not let you be tempted beyond what you can bear. But when you are tempted, he will also provide a way out so that you can endure it." By relying on God's strength and seeking His guidance through prayer and Scripture, you can develop the self-control needed to overcome temptation.

Moreover, Samson's story highlights the importance of accountability and surrounding yourself with positive influences. If Samson had been accountable to godly friends or mentors, they might have helped him recognize and avoid the temptations that ultimately led to his downfall. As you navigate the challenges of teenage life, seek out friends and mentors who will encourage you in your faith and hold you accountable to God's standards.

Reflection

• *In what areas of your life do you struggle with self-control, and how can you rely on God's strength to overcome temptation?*

• *How can you guard your heart and mind against negative influences and temptations?*

• *Who are the godly friends and mentors in your life who can provide accountability and support as you strive to live a life pleasing to God?*

Prayer

Dear God, thank You for the lessons we can learn from Samson's life. Help us to develop self-control and to rely on Your strength when we face temptation. Give us wisdom to guard our hearts and minds, and surround us with godly influences who will encourage us in our faith. Amen.

14

HANNAH AND SAMUEL

___ / ___ / _____

*"As each has received a gift, use it to serve one another, as
good stewards of God's varied grace."*

— 1 PETER 4:10

*H*annah was a woman who deeply desired to have a
child, but she was unable to conceive. Year after year,
she would go to the temple to pray and pour out her heart to God.
One day, Hannah made a vow to God, saying that if He would grant
her a son, she would dedicate the child to His service. God heard
Hannah's prayer and blessed her with a son, whom she named
Samuel.

True to her word, Hannah kept her promise to God. After Samuel
was weaned, she brought him to the temple to serve under Eli, the
high priest. Hannah's prayer of thanksgiving reveals her deep gratitude and understanding that Samuel was a gift from God, and she
was entrusting him back to God's service. (Samuel Chapters 1 to 2)

IN THE STORY of found in the book of I Samuel 1-2, we encounter the inspiring story of Hannah, a woman who exemplified what it means to be a good steward of the gifts God has given us.

It's easy to take things for granted or to believe that what we have is solely the result of our own efforts. However, Hannah's example reminds us that everything we have is ultimately a gift from God, and we are called to use those gifts to honor and serve Him.

Being a good steward means recognizing that our time, talents, and resources are not our own, but rather, they are entrusted to us by God to use for His purposes. Like Hannah, who dedicated her long-awaited son to God's service, we can ask ourselves how we can use the blessings in our lives to glorify God and make a positive impact on others.

For example, if you have a talent for music, you could use that gift to lead worship or to share uplifting songs with those who are struggling. If you have been blessed with financial resources, you could practice generosity by giving to those in need or supporting ministries that advance God's kingdom. If you have been given the gift of time, you could volunteer in your church or community, using your skills and energy to serve others.

Moreover, being a good steward involves cultivating a heart of gratitude and trust in God. Hannah's prayer in I Samuel 2 is a beautiful example of someone who recognized God's goodness and faithfulness, even in the midst of her own challenges. By nurturing a thankful heart and trusting in God's plan for your life, you can experience the joy and peace that comes from living as a faithful steward.

Reflection

• *What are some of the gifts and blessings God has given you, and how can you use them to honor Him and serve others?*

• *In what areas of your life do you struggle to trust God and surrender control to Him? How can Hannah's example encourage you to trust in God's plan?*

• *How can you cultivate a heart of gratitude and thankfulness, even in the midst of life's challenges and difficulties?*

Prayer

Dear God, thank You for the example of Hannah and the reminder that everything we have is a gift from You. Help us to be good stewards of the blessings You have given us, using them to honor You and serve others. Grant us hearts of gratitude and trust, as we seek to follow Your plan for our lives. Amen.

15

DAVID AND GOLIATH

___ / ___ / _____

"When I am afraid, I put my trust in you. In God, whose word I praise—in God I trust and am not afraid. What can mere mortals do to me?"

— PSALM 56:3-4

The Philistines and the Israelites were gathered for battle, with the Philistines on one hill and the Israelites on another, and a valley between them. A giant named Goliath, from the city of Gath, came out of the Philistine camp. He was over nine feet tall and wore heavy bronze armor. Goliath challenged the Israelites to send out a champion to face him in single combat, taunting them and their God.

For forty days, Goliath came forward and issued his challenge, but no Israelite dared to fight him. One day, Jesse sent his youngest son, David, to the battle lines to bring food to his older brothers and check on them. When David arrived, he heard Goliath's challenge and saw the fear in the Israelite men. David volunteered to fight the giant, despite being just a young shepherd boy.

King Saul was skeptical but allowed David to face Goliath. David refused Saul's armor and sword, opting instead for his sling and five smooth stones from a nearby brook. As Goliath approached, cursing David and his God, David ran towards him, declaring that the battle belonged to the Lord. David slung a stone, striking Goliath in the forehead. The giant fell face down, and David cut off his head with Goliath's own sword.

Seeing their champion defeated, the Philistines fled, and the Israelites pursued them, winning a great victory. David's faith and courage, despite the odds, allowed him to triumph over Goliath and bring victory to his people. (1 Samuel Chapter 17)

DAVID'S STORY is a powerful reminder that no matter how big our fears or challenges may seem, we can overcome them with faith in God. As teenagers, you face many "giants" in your lives - academic pressure, social anxiety, family conflicts, self-doubt, and more. It's easy to feel overwhelmed and afraid, just like the Israelites who were terrified of Goliath.

However, David's example shows us that when we put our trust in God, we can face our fears with courage and confidence. David didn't rely on his own strength or abilities; he knew that his victory would come from God alone. By stepping out in faith, David not only defeated Goliath but also inspired his fellow Israelites to trust in God's power.

In your own lives, you can follow David's example by turning to God when you feel afraid or overwhelmed. Through prayer, reading the Bible, and seeking godly counsel, you can cultivate a deep faith that will sustain you through life's challenges. Remember, God is always with you, and He has promised to give you strength and courage when you need it most.

Moreover, David's story teaches us the importance of perspective. While the Israelites saw Goliath as an invincible giant, David saw him as just another obstacle that God could help him overcome. When you face your own "giants," try to see them from God's perspective. Trust that God is bigger than your fears and that He can use even the most daunting challenges to grow your faith and character.

Reflection

• *What are some of the "giants" or fears that you face in your life, and how can you trust God to help you overcome them?*

• *How can you cultivate a deeper faith in God, like David's, that will give you courage and confidence in the face of challenges?*

• *In what ways can you encourage others who are facing their own fears and struggles, sharing the hope and strength that comes from trusting in God?*

Prayer

Dear God, thank You for the example of David and the reminder that we can overcome fear with faith in You. When we face challenges that seem insurmountable, help us to trust in Your power and goodness. Give us the courage to step out in faith, knowing that You are always with us. Amen.

•

16

THE STORY OF ABIGAIL

___ / ___ / _____

"Blessed are the peacemakers, for they will be called children of God."

— MATTHEW 5:9

*D*avid, not yet king, was living in the wilderness with his
men, protecting the local shepherds and their flocks. One
of these shepherds was a wealthy but ill-tempered man named
Nabal. When David sent his men to ask for provisions, Nabal rudely
refused, despite David's protection of his shepherds. Angered by this
insult, David set out with his men to take revenge on Nabal. However,
one of Nabal's servants informed Nabal's wife, Abigail, of the situation. Abigail, described as intelligent and beautiful, quickly gathered
a generous supply of food and set out to meet David, without telling
her husband.

When Abigail met David, she humbly apologized for her husband's
behavior and pleaded with David not to shed blood or take revenge.
She acknowledged David as the future king of Israel and urged him
not to have the guilt of needless bloodshed on his conscience.

Abigail's wise words and timely intervention diffused David's anger, and he accepted her gifts and heeded her advice. When Abigail returned home, she found Nabal drunk from a feast. The next morning, when she told him about her meeting with David, Nabal's heart failed, and he became paralyzed. About ten days later, the Lord struck Nabal, and he died.

Upon hearing of Nabal's death, David praised God for keeping him from unnecessary violence and sent for Abigail to become his wife. Abigail's wisdom, humility, and decisive action saved her household and won David's respect and admiration. (1 Samuel Chapter 25)

ABIGAIL'S STORY is a powerful example of the importance of being a peacemaker. As teenagers, you may face conflicts and tensions in your relationships with friends, family members, or classmates. It's easy to get caught up in the heat of the moment and react with anger or retaliation, but Abigail's example shows us a better way.

Being a peacemaker means actively seeking to resolve conflicts and promote understanding, even when it's difficult or unpopular. Like Abigail, who risked her own safety to prevent bloodshed, peacemakers are willing to step out of their comfort zones and take bold action to bring reconciliation.

Moreover, Abigail's story teaches us the value of wisdom and humility in resolving conflicts. Instead of defending her husband's foolish behavior, Abigail acknowledged his wrongdoing and appealed to David's sense of justice and mercy. By approaching the situation with wisdom and tact, Abigail was able to diffuse David's anger and prevent a tragic outcome.

As you navigate the challenges of teenage life, remember that God has called you to be a peacemaker. This doesn't mean avoiding conflict altogether or compromising your values, but rather, it means actively seeking to bring healing and reconciliation in your relationships. By relying on God's wisdom and grace, you can be an agent of peace in your family, school, and community.

Reflection

• *In what relationships or situations do you find it most challenging to be a peacemaker, and how can you ask God for wisdom and courage to promote reconciliation?*

• *How can you cultivate the qualities of humility, wisdom, and boldness that Abigail demonstrated in her interaction with David?*

• *In what ways can your commitment to being a peacemaker reflect the love and grace of Christ to those around you?*

Prayer

Dear God, thank You for the example of Abigail and the reminder that we are called to be peacemakers. Give us the wisdom, humility, and courage to seek reconciliation in our relationships and to be agents of Your love and grace in the world. May our lives bring glory to You as we strive to promote peace and understanding. Amen.

17

JOSHUA'S TREATY WITH THE GIBEONITES

___ / ___ / _____

"[The one] who keeps an oath even when it hurts, and does not change their mind."

— PSALM 15:4

*A*fter Joshua led the Israelites to victories over Jericho and Ai, the kings west of the Jordan gathered to fight against Israel. However, when the people of Gibeon, a large city, heard what Joshua had done to Jericho and Ai, they resorted to deception to save themselves. The Gibeonites dressed in worn-out clothes and took old, dry provisions to make it seem like they had traveled a great distance. They went to Joshua at his camp in Gilgal and claimed to be from a far country, seeking to make a peace treaty with Israel. The Israelites were suspicious and asked if the Gibeonites lived nearby, but they insisted they were from a distant land. Joshua and the leaders of Israel did not seek the Lord's guidance and instead made a peace treaty with the Gibeonites, swearing an oath to let them live.

Three days later, the Israelites discovered that the Gibeonites were actually their neighbors. Despite the deception, the Israelite leaders refused to break their oath, but they made the Gibeonites woodcutters and water carriers for the congregation and the altar of the Lord. When the king of Jerusalem heard that Gibeon had made peace with Israel, he and four other Amorite kings attacked Gibeon. The Gibeonites sent to Joshua for help, and Joshua, with the Lord's assurance of victory, marched all night to aid them. The Lord threw the Amorite armies into confusion, and Joshua pursued and defeated them with the help of a divinely sent hailstorm. (Joshua Chapter 9)

JOSHUA'S STORY teaches us the importance of honoring our commitments, even when it's difficult or inconvenient. As teenagers, you may face situations where you make promises or commitments to others, whether it's to a friend, a family member, a teacher, or a coach. It's easy to make promises in the moment, but following through on those commitments takes integrity and responsibility.

When Joshua and the Israelite leaders realized they had been deceived, they could have easily justified breaking their treaty with the Gibeonites. However, they recognized that their word and their oath before God were sacred, and they had to honor their commitment, even if it meant facing the consequences of their mistake.

In your own life, honoring commitments means being true to your word and following through on what you've promised, even when it's challenging or requires sacrifice. It means being reliable and trustworthy, and showing others that they can count on you to do what you say you'll do.

Moreover, Joshua's story reminds us of the importance of seeking God's guidance before making important decisions or commitments. Had Joshua and the leaders consulted God first, they may have avoided the deception and the resulting complications. As you navigate the choices and commitments of teenage life, make it a habit to pray and seek God's wisdom, trusting that He will guide you in the right path.

Reflection

• *In what areas of your life do you struggle with honoring commitments, and how can you ask God for strength and integrity to follow through on your word?*

• *How can you cultivate the habit of seeking God's guidance before making important decisions or commitments?*

• *In what ways can your commitment to honoring your word be a witness to others and demonstrate the character of Christ?*

Prayer

Dear God, thank You for Joshua's example of honoring commitments. Help us to be people of integrity, true to our word and guided by Your wisdom in all our decisions. Give us the strength to do what is right, even when it's difficult. May our lives reflect Your faithfulness and bring glory to Your name. Amen.

18

NEHEMIAH REBUILDS THE WALLS

___ / ___ / _____

"Iron sharpens iron, and one man sharpens another."

— PROVERBS 27:17

*N*ehemiah, a Jew serving as cupbearer to the Persian king Artaxerxes, received word that the walls of Jerusalem were in ruins and the people were in distress. Deeply troubled, Nehemiah prayed to God, confessing the sins of Israel and asking for favor in his quest to rebuild the city. Artaxerxes noticed Nehemiah's sadness and asked the reason. Nehemiah requested permission to return to Jerusalem and rebuild the city walls. The king granted his request, providing letters of safe conduct and resources for the project.

Upon arriving in Jerusalem, Nehemiah surveyed the damage to the walls and rallied the people to start rebuilding. He assigned sections of the wall to different families and groups, and the work began in earnest. However, the project faced opposition from local officials, Sanballat and Tobiah, who mocked and threatened the builders. Undeterred, Nehemiah stationed guards and armed the workers, encouraging them to trust in God. As the work progressed, Sanballat and his allies plotted to attack Jerusalem and stop the rebuilding.

Nehemiah again turned to prayer and posted guards day and night. He also addressed issues of social injustice among the Jews, ensuring that the poor were not exploited during this time. Despite the challenges, the wall was completed in just 52 days. Nehemiah then organized the people, ensuring that the city was well-populated and that the Levites were supported in their temple duties. He also led the people in renewing their covenant with God and celebrating the Feast of Tabernacles. (The book of Nehemia)

NEHEMIAH'S STORY teaches us the value of teamwork and the incredible things that can be accomplished when people work together towards a common goal. As teenagers, you have many opportunities to be part of a team, whether it's in sports, school projects, church ministries, or community service.

Being a good team player means recognizing that everyone has unique skills, strengths, and perspectives to contribute. Just as each family in Jerusalem was assigned a specific section of the wall to repair, each member of a team has a role to play in achieving the overall mission. By valuing and leveraging each person's abilities, teams can accomplish far more than any individual could alone.

Moreover, Nehemiah's story highlights the importance of leadership and encouragement in teamwork. Nehemiah not only organized the people and assigned tasks, but he also motivated them with his words and his own example of hard work and dedication. As a team member, you can be a source of encouragement and support for your teammates, cheering them on and helping them stay focused on the goal.

In your own life, look for opportunities to be part of a team and to cultivate teamwork skills. Whether it's collaborating on a school project, serving together in a church outreach, or participating in a sports team, approach teamwork with a spirit of humility, cooperation, and enthusiasm. Remember that by working together and supporting one another, you can achieve great things and make a positive impact in your community and the world.

Reflection

• *What are some of the teams or groups you are currently part of, and how can you contribute your unique skills and strengths to help the team succeed?*

• *How can you be a source of encouragement and support for your teammates, especially when facing challenges or opposition?*

• *In what ways can your participation in teamwork be a witness to others and demonstrate the love and unity of Christ?*

Prayer

Dear God, thank You for the example of Nehemiah and the value of teamwork. Help us to recognize and appreciate the unique gifts and abilities of others, and to work together in humility and cooperation. Give us the courage to be leaders and encouragers, and to pursue Your purposes through collaborative efforts. May our teamwork bring glory to You and bless those around us. Amen.

HELP OTHERS DISCOVER GOD'S WISDOM

"As iron sharpens iron, so one person sharpens another."

— PROVERBS 27:17

*Y*ou've made it halfway through "*10-Minute Bible Stories for Teens*," and I hope you're already discovering the power of God's wisdom and love. As you continue on this journey, I have a special request for you.

Would you take a moment to consider helping another teenager, just like you, find the same inspiration and guidance that you're uncovering in these pages?

Your review, once you've finished the book, could be the very thing that encourages another young person to embark on their own journey of faith and self-discovery.

By sharing your thoughts, you'll be joining a community of young believers who are making a difference in the world. You'll be showing others that they're not alone and that there's hope and purpose to be found in God's love.

When you've turned the final page, please take a few minutes to leave your honest review by scanning the QR code below. Your words will be a blessing to someone you may never meet but who will be forever grateful for your kindness.

SCAN ME

Thank you for being a part of this journey. I can't wait to see how your review will inspire and encourage other young people to seek God's wisdom and guidance.

May God bless you abundantly as you continue to grow in faith and share His love with the world.

With gratitude,

Biblical Teachings

P.S. - Remember, when you share something valuable with others, you become even more valuable to them. If you know another teenager who could benefit from this book, please consider sharing it with them once you've finished reading. You never know how God might use your generosity to change a life!

New Testament

1 9

THE PARABLE OF THE THREE SERVANTS

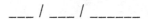

"Those who work their land will have abundant food, but those who chase fantasies have no sense."

— PROVERBS 12:11

A man, going on a journey, called his servants and entrusted his property to them. To one he gave five talents, to another two, and to another one, each according to his ability. The servant who received five talents traded with them and made five talents more. Likewise, the one with two talents made two more. But the servant who received one talent dug in the ground and hid his master's money.

After a long time, the master returned and settled accounts with his servants. The servant with five talents brought five more, and his master commended him, giving him charge over many things and inviting him to share his joy. The servant with two talents did likewise and received the same commendation and reward.

However, the servant who had received one talent said, "Master, I knew you to be a hard man, reaping where you did not sow, so I was afraid and hid your talent in the ground. Here, you have what is yours." The master rebuked him as a wicked and slothful servant, saying that he should have invested the money with the bankers to earn interest. The master ordered the talent to be taken from him and given to the one with ten talents, stating that to everyone who has, more will be given, but from the one who has not, even what he has will be taken away. The worthless servant was cast into the outer darkness. (Matthew Chapter 25)

THE PARABLE OF the talents teaches us that God has given each of us unique gifts, abilities, and resources, and He expects us to use them diligently and responsibly for His purposes. As teenagers, you may be tempted to compare your talents to others or to underestimate the value of what God has entrusted to you. But this parable reminds us that it's not about the amount of talents we have, but rather how faithfully we use and multiply them.

Hard work is a crucial aspect of stewarding our talents well. The servants who invested their talents and put them to work were praised and rewarded by their master. They didn't sit back and wait for opportunities to come to them, but actively sought ways to use and grow what they had been given. In the same way, God calls us to be proactive and diligent in developing and using our talents for His glory and the good of others.

This may mean putting in the time and effort to cultivate a skill or ability, whether it's in academics, sports, music, or another area. It may involve stepping out in faith to serve in a ministry or volunteer opportunity, even when it stretches you beyond your comfort zone. It may require perseverance and resilience in the face of challenges or setbacks, trusting that God is at work in and through your efforts.

The parable also warns against the dangers of fear and laziness. The servant who buried his talent did so out of fear of failure and a desire to play it safe. But in the end, his inaction and lack of effort were rebuked by the master. As you navigate the pressures and uncertainties of teenage life, don't let fear hold you back from using your talents and taking risks for God's kingdom. Trust that as you step out in faith and work diligently, God will be with you and will multiply your efforts for His purposes.

Reflection

• *What are the unique talents, gifts, and resources God has entrusted to you? How can you cultivate and use them more fully for His glory?*

• *In what areas of your life do you struggle with fear, laziness, or a desire to play it safe? How can you challenge yourself to step out in faith and work diligently, even when it's difficult?*

• *How can your hard work and faithful stewardship of your talents be a witness to others and point them to the goodness and generosity of God?*

Prayer

Heavenly Father, thank You for the gifts, talents, and resources You have entrusted to us. Help us to be diligent and faithful stewards, putting to work what You have given us for Your glory and the good of others. Give us the courage to step out in faith, the perseverance to work hard, and the joy of knowing that our efforts are multiplied by Your grace. May our lives reflect Your goodness and generosity to the world around us. In Jesus' name, Amen.

20

THE TEMPTATION OF CHRIST

___ / ___ / _____

*"Watch and pray so that you will not fall into temptation.
The spirit is willing, but the flesh is weak."*

— MATTHEW 26:41

*A*fter being baptized by John, Jesus was led by the Spirit into the wilderness to be tempted by the devil. He fasted for forty days and forty nights, and afterward, he was hungry.

The tempter came to him and said, "If you are the Son of God, command these stones to become loaves of bread." But Jesus answered, "It is written, 'Man shall not live by bread alone, but by every word that comes from the mouth of God.'"

Then the devil took him to the holy city and set him on the pinnacle of the temple, saying, "If you are the Son of God, throw yourself down, for it is written, 'He will command his angels concerning you,' and 'On their hands they will bear you up, lest you strike your foot against a stone.'" Jesus replied, "Again it is written, 'You shall not put the Lord your God to the test.'"

Finally, the devil took him to a very high mountain and showed him all the kingdoms of the world and their glory, saying, "All these I will give you, if you will fall down and worship me." But Jesus said to him, "Be gone, Satan! For it is written, 'You shall worship the Lord your God and him only shall you serve.'"

Then the devil left him, and behold, angels came and were ministering to him. (Books of Matthew and Luke)

As TEENS, you face numerous temptations in your daily lives. These can range from the pressure to fit in with your peers, the desire to engage in risky behaviors, or the struggle to maintain integrity in your academic and personal pursuits. The story of Jesus' temptation reminds us that everyone, even the Son of God, faces temptation, but we have the power to overcome it through faith and reliance on God's word.

When you find yourself in situations where you are tempted to compromise your values or make poor choices, remember to turn to Scripture for guidance and strength. Just as Jesus used God's word to counter the devil's temptations, you can use biblical principles to navigate difficult decisions and remain faithful to your beliefs.

For example, if you are tempted to cheat on a test or lie to your parents, recall verses that emphasize the importance of honesty and integrity, such as Proverbs 10:9, "Whoever walks in integrity walks securely, but whoever takes crooked paths will be found out." By applying these truths to your life, you can build a strong foundation of character and resist the pull of temptation.

Reflection

• *What are some common temptations you face as a teenager? How can you use God's word and prayer to overcome these temptations?*

• *Reflect on a time when you successfully resisted temptation. What strategies or resources helped you in that moment, and how can you apply them to future situations?*

• *How can you support and encourage your friends or peers who may be struggling with temptation? What practical steps can you take to create a culture of accountability and mutual support?*

Prayer

Dear God, thank you for the example of Jesus and his victory over temptation. Give me the wisdom to recognize temptation in my life and the strength to resist it through the power of your word. Help me to rely on you in every moment, and to lead a life that honors you. Amen.

21

THE CLEANSING OF A LEPER

___ / ___ / _____

"Be kind and compassionate to one another, forgiving each other, just as in Christ God forgave you."

— EPHESIANS 4:32

A man with leprosy came to Jesus, begging on his knees and saying, "If you are willing, you can make me clean." In those days, leprosy was a highly contagious and incurable skin disease that led to isolation and social stigma. Lepers were considered unclean and were forced to live outside of the community, separated from their loved ones.

Moved with compassion, Jesus reached out His hand and touched the man, saying, "I am willing. Be clean!" Immediately, the leprosy left the man, and he was cleansed. Jesus then instructed him to go and show himself to the priest and offer the sacrifices Moses commanded for his cleansing as a testimony.

However, the man went out and began to talk freely about what had happened, spreading the news far and wide. As a result, Jesus could no longer enter a town openly but stayed outside in lonely places. Yet the people still came to Him from everywhere. (Mark Chapter 1)

THE STORY of Jesus healing the leper teaches us the importance of showing compassion to others, especially those who are marginalized, suffering, or in need. As teenagers, you may encounter people in your school, community, or online who are dealing with physical, emotional, or social challenges. Maybe it's a classmate who is being bullied, a friend who is struggling with mental health issues, or a homeless person you pass on the street.

In a world that often prioritizes self-interest and personal comfort, Jesus' example of compassion stands out as a radical call to love and serve others. He didn't shy away from the leper's suffering or the potential risk of infection. Instead, He reached out and touched the man, demonstrating His willingness to enter into his pain and offer healing and restoration.

As followers of Christ, we are called to extend that same compassion to those around us. This doesn't necessarily mean performing miraculous healings, but rather, it means being willing to step into others' lives with empathy, kindness, and practical support. It means looking beyond the surface level and seeking to understand the struggles and needs of those who are hurting.

Showing compassion may involve listening to someone's story without judgment, offering words of encouragement, or providing tangible assistance like a meal or a ride to the doctor's office. It may mean advocating for those who are marginalized or oppressed, using your voice and influence to bring about positive change in your school or community.

Remember, when you show compassion to others, you are reflecting the heart of Jesus and demonstrating the power of His love to a watching world. Your acts of kindness and care, no matter how small they may seem, can have a profound impact on someone's life and can open the door for them to experience the transformative love of Christ.

Reflection

• *Who are the people in your life who may be in need of compassion and support? How can you reach out to them with empathy and practical care?*

• *In what situations do you find it most challenging to show compassion, and how can you ask God for the grace and strength to love others as He does?*

• *How can your acts of compassion be a witness to others and point them to the love and healing power of Jesus?*

Prayer

Heavenly Father, thank You for Jesus' compassion. Help us see others through Your eyes and reach out with empathy and support. Give us courage to help the hurting and be instruments of Your love and healing. May our actions show the power of Your grace. In Jesus' name, Amen.

22

THE WIDOW'S OFFERING

___ / ___ / _____

*"Give, and it will be given to you. A good measure, pressed
down, shaken together and running over, will be poured
into your lap. For with the measure you use, it will be
measured to you."*

— LUKE 6:38

One day, Jesus was sitting near the temple treasury, observing people as they placed their offerings into the collection box. Many wealthy individuals put in large sums of money, drawing attention to their substantial gifts. However, amidst the crowd, a poor widow approached the box and quietly dropped in two small copper coins, worth only a fraction of a penny.

Jesus called His disciples to Him and pointed out the widow's offering, saying, "Truly I tell you, this poor widow has put more into the treasury than all the others. They all gave out of their wealth; but she, out of her poverty, put in everything—all she had to live on" (Mark Chapter 12)

THE STORY of the poor widow's offering teaches us that true giving is not measured by the amount we give, but by the heart and sacrifice behind it. As teenagers, you may feel like you don't have much to offer, whether it's in terms of money, talents, or resources. You may compare yourself to others who seem to have more to give or who receive recognition for their contributions.

But the poor widow's example shows us that the value of our giving is not determined by the size of our gift, but by the depth of our devotion and the willingness to give all that we have. She gave not out of her abundance, but out of her poverty, trusting that God would provide for her needs.

Giving with a joyful and sacrificial heart is an act of worship and faith. It demonstrates our trust in God's provision and our desire to be a part of His work in the world. When we give generously, not just from our excess but from our very substance, we experience the joy and freedom that comes from aligning our hearts with God's heart for generosity and compassion.

Moreover, the poor widow's story reminds us that our giving is not just about meeting the needs of others, but about the condition of our own hearts. Jesus commended the widow not because her gift made a significant financial impact, but because it reflected a heart fully surrendered to God. As you consider your own giving, whether it's your time, talents, or resources, ask yourself what your giving reveals about your priorities and your relationship with God.

Remember, no gift is too small or insignificant when it is given with a heart of love and obedience. As you navigate the challenges and opportunities of teenage life, look for ways to give joyfully and sacrificially, trusting that God will use your offerings to bless others and grow you in your faith.

Reflection

• *In what areas of your life can you practice joyful and sacrificial giving, even if you feel like you don't have much to offer?*

• *How can you cultivate a heart of generosity and trust in God's provision, rather than holding onto your resources out of fear or selfish ambition?*

• *In what ways can your giving, both in attitude and action, be a witness to others of God's love and generosity?*

Prayer

Heavenly Father, thank You for the example of the poor widow and her true giving. Help us give joyfully and sacrificially from our substance, not our excess. Teach us to trust in Your provision and align our hearts with Yours. May our giving be an act of worship and reflect Your generosity. In Jesus' name, Amen.

23

THE GOOD SAMARITAN

___ / ___ / _____

"You, my brothers and sisters, were called to be free. But do not use your freedom to indulge the flesh; rather, serve one another humbly in love."

— GALATIANS 5:13

A lawyer stood up to test Jesus, asking, "Teacher, what shall I do to inherit eternal life?" Jesus responded by asking the lawyer what was written in the law. The lawyer answered, "Love the Lord your God with all your heart, soul, strength, and mind, and love your neighbor as yourself." Jesus confirmed that this was correct and told the lawyer to do this to live. Seeking to justify himself, the lawyer asked, "And who is my neighbor?" In response, Jesus told a parable:

A man was going down from Jerusalem to Jericho when he fell among robbers. They stripped him, beat him, and left him half dead. A priest happened to be going down that road, but when he saw the man, he passed by on the other side. Similarly, a Levite came to the place, saw the man, and passed by on the other side. But a Samaritan, as he journeyed, came to where the man was. When he saw him, he had compassion. He went to him, bound up his wounds, pouring on oil and wine. Then he set the man on his own animal, brought him to an inn, and took care of him. The next day, he took out two denarii, gave them to the innkeeper, and said, "Take care of him, and whatever more you spend, I will repay you when I come back."

Jesus then asked the lawyer, "Which of these three, do you think, proved to be a neighbor to the man who fell among the robbers?" The lawyer said, "The one who showed him mercy." And Jesus said to him, "You go, and do likewise." (Luke Chapter 10)

THE PARABLE OF the Good Samaritan teaches us that serving others with kindness means extending compassion and care to all people, regardless of their background, social status, or relationship to us. As teenagers, you have countless opportunities to practice kindness and make a positive impact on those around you.

In a world that often prioritizes self-interest and personal gain, the Good Samaritan's actions stand out as a radical example of selfless love. He didn't hesitate to stop and help a stranger in need, even though it required time, effort, and resources. He saw someone who was hurting and responded with practical, hands-on assistance.

As you navigate the challenges and pressures of teenage life, it's easy to become focused on your own needs and desires. But Jesus calls us to a different way of living - one that puts others first and seeks to serve rather than be served. This means being attentive to the needs of those around you, whether it's a classmate who is struggling, a friend who is going through a tough time, or a stranger who could use a helping hand.

Serving others with kindness may involve stepping out of your comfort zone or sacrificing your own interests for the sake of someone else. It may mean befriending the lonely, standing up for the bullied, or volunteering your time and talents to make a difference in your community. But as you extend kindness and compassion to others, you reflect the heart of Christ and experience the joy and fulfillment that comes from living a life of purpose.

Reflection

• *Who are the people in your life who may be in need of kindness and compassion? How can you practically serve and support them?*

• *In what ways do you struggle to extend kindness to those who are different from you or who may be considered "outsiders"? How can you challenge yourself to love and serve others as the Good Samaritan did?*

• *How can your acts of kindness and service be a witness to others and point them to the love and compassion of Christ?*

Prayer

Heavenly Father, thank You for the Good Samaritan's example. Open our eyes to others' needs and give us the courage to serve with kindness and compassion. Help us extend kindness to everyone, reflecting Your heart. May our lives show generosity, selflessness, and practical care for others. In Jesus' name, Amen.

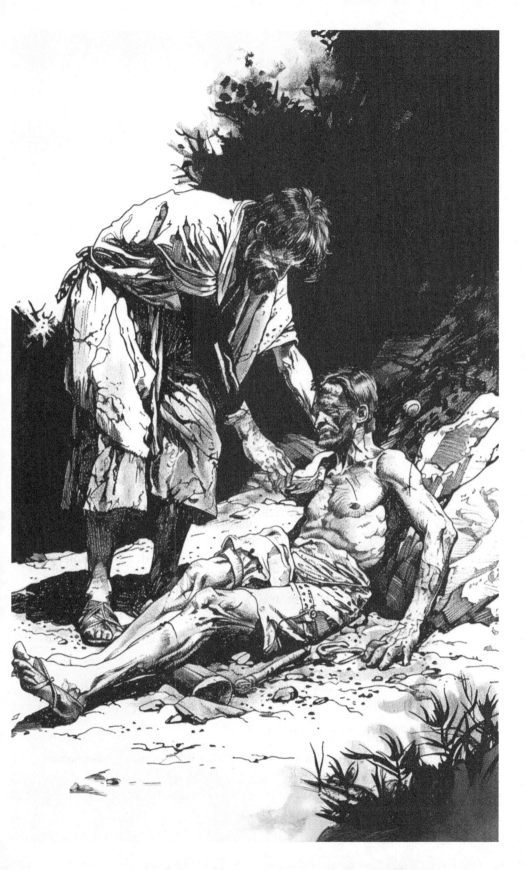

24

THE WOMAN WHO ANOINTED
JESUS' FEET

___ / ___ / _____

*"Do nothing out of selfish ambition or vain conceit. Rather,
in humility value others above yourselves, not looking
to your own interests but each of you to the interests of
the others."*

— PHILIPPIANS 2:3-4

a Pharisee named Simon invited Jesus to eat with him. Jesus entered the Pharisee's house and reclined at the table. A woman in the city, who was a sinner, learned that Jesus was dining there. She brought an alabaster flask of ointment and stood behind him at his feet, weeping. She began to wet his feet with her tears and wiped them with the hair of her head. Then she kissed his feet and anointed them with the ointment.

When the Pharisee saw this, he said to himself, "If this man were a prophet, he would have known who and what sort of woman this is who is touching him, for she is a sinner."

Jesus, answering the Pharisee's thoughts, said, "Simon, I have something to say to you." Simon replied, "Say it, Teacher." Jesus then told a parable of two debtors: one owed five hundred denarii, and the other fifty. When they could not pay, the moneylender cancelled the debt of both. Jesus asked Simon which debtor would love the moneylender more. Simon answered, "The one, I suppose, for whom he cancelled the larger debt." Jesus affirmed that Simon had judged rightly.

Turning toward the woman, Jesus said to Simon, "Do you see this woman? I entered your house; you gave me no water for my feet, but she has wet my feet with her tears and wiped them with her hair. You gave me no kiss, but from the time I came in, she has not ceased to kiss my feet. You did not anoint my head with oil, but she has anointed my feet with ointment. Therefore, I tell you, her sins, which are many, are forgiven—for she loved much. But he who is forgiven little, loves little."

Jesus said to the woman, "Your sins are forgiven." Those who were at table with him began to say among themselves, "Who is this, who even forgives sins?" But Jesus said to the woman, "Your faith has saved you; go in peace." (Luke Chapter 7)

THE STORY of Jesus dining at Simon's home teaches us the value of good manners and the importance of extending grace and hospitality to others. As teenagers, you may sometimes feel like manners and etiquette are old-fashioned or unnecessary, especially in a world that often prioritizes informality and self-expression. However, good manners are about more than just following rules or impressing others; they are a way of showing respect, kindness, and consideration for those around us.

In the story, Simon failed to show Jesus the basic courtesies expected of a host, such as providing water for His feet or a kiss of greeting. His lack of good manners revealed a deeper heart issue: a lack of love and respect for Jesus. In contrast, the woman who anointed Jesus' feet demonstrated extraordinary love and devotion, even though she was looked down upon by others because of her sinful past.

As followers of Christ, we are called to extend grace, hospitality, and respect to all people, regardless of their background or social status. This means taking the time to learn and practice good manners, such as saying "please" and "thank you," listening attentively when others are speaking, and showing appreciation for the kindnesses shown to us.

Good manners are also a way of putting others' needs and comfort above our own. When we choose to use polite language, to listen more than we speak, or to offer a helping hand, we demonstrate the love and humility of Christ. These small acts of consideration can make a significant impact on those around us, creating a culture of respect and kindness.

Moreover, the story reminds us that our manners and actions often reflect the state of our hearts. When we prioritize showing love and honor to others, it is a sign that we have experienced the grace and forgiveness of God in our own lives. As you seek to grow in your faith and character, ask God to shape your heart and to help you express His love through your words and actions.

Reflection

• *In what situations or relationships do you find it most challenging to practice good manners, and how can you ask God for the grace and wisdom to respond with kindness and respect?*

• *How can you make a habit of putting others' needs and comfort above your own, even in small everyday interactions?*

• *In what ways can your good manners and gracious behavior be a witness to others of the love and humility of Christ?*

Prayer

Heavenly Father, thank You for the example of the woman who anointed Jesus' feet. Help us to express love and honor through our actions, showing grace, hospitality, and respect to all. Give us hearts that prioritize others' needs and reflect Christ's love and humility in our words and actions. In Jesus' name, Amen.

25

THE HEALING OF JARIUS' DAUGHTER

___ / ___ / _____

"But from everlasting to everlasting the Lord's love is with those who fear him, and his righteousness with their children's children."

— PSALM 103:17

When Jesus returned from the region of the Gerasenes, a large crowd gathered around him. Jairus, a ruler of the synagogue, came and fell at Jesus' feet, earnestly pleading with him to come to his house because his only daughter, about twelve years old, was dying.

As Jesus went with Jairus, the crowds pressed around him. A woman who had suffered from a discharge of blood for twelve years and had spent all her living on physicians without being healed came up behind Jesus and touched the fringe of his garment. Immediately, her discharge of blood ceased, and she felt in her body that she was healed. Jesus, perceiving that power had gone out from him, asked who had touched him. The woman, knowing what had happened to her, came in fear and trembling, fell down before him, and declared in the presence of all the people why she had touched him and how she had been immediately healed. Jesus said to her, "Daughter, your faith has made you well; go in peace."

While Jesus was still speaking, someone from Jairus' house came and said, "Your daughter is dead. Do not trouble the Teacher any more." But Jesus, hearing this, said to Jairus, "Do not fear; only believe, and she will be well."

When Jesus came to Jairus' house, he allowed no one to enter with him except Peter, James, John, and the child's father and mother. People were weeping and mourning for the girl, but Jesus said, "Do not weep, for she is not dead but sleeping." They laughed at him, knowing that she was dead. But taking her by the hand, Jesus called, saying, "Child, arise." Her spirit returned, and she got up at once. He directed that something should be given her to eat and amazed her parents, but he charged them to tell no one what had happened. (Books of Luke and Mark)

As TEENS, your family plays a crucial role in your life, providing love, support, and guidance as you navigate the challenges of growing up. The story of Jairus and his daughter highlights the deep, unconditional love that parents have for their children and the lengths they will go to ensure their well-being.

It's important to recognize and celebrate the love within your family, even amidst the ups and downs of daily life. Take time to express your appreciation for your parents, siblings, and extended family members. Share your joys, struggles, and dreams with them, and be open to their wisdom and encouragement.

In moments of difficulty or crisis, remember that your family is a source of strength and that you can turn to them for support, just as Jairus turned to Jesus in his time of need. By nurturing and celebrating the love within your family, you create a strong foundation for your own personal growth and faith journey.

Reflection

• *Think about a time when your family showed you unconditional love and support. How did that experience impact you, and how can you extend that same love to others?*

• *What are some practical ways you can express your appreciation and celebrate the love within your family? Consider acts of kindness, quality time together, or heartfelt conversations.*

• *How can you lean on your family's love and support during challenging times, while also deepening your trust in God's plan for your life?*

Prayer

Dear God, thank you for the gift of family and the love we share. Help me to cherish and celebrate the relationships you have placed in my life. In times of joy and sorrow, may I always remember the power of unconditional love and the importance of faith in you. Amen.

26

THE PARABLE OF THE PRODIGAL SON

___ / ___ / _____

"But God shows his love for us in that while we were still sinners, Christ died for us."

— ROMANS 5:8

*J*esus told a parable about a man who had two sons. The younger son asked his father to give him his share of the inheritance. The father agreed and divided his property between the two sons. The younger son took his wealth and traveled to a distant country, where he squandered his money on wild living. When a famine struck the land, he found himself in need and took a job feeding pigs. He was so hungry that he longed to eat the pigs' food, but no one gave him anything. Finally, the son came to his senses and realized that even his father's hired servants had more than enough to eat. He decided to return home, confess his sins, and ask his father to treat him as a hired servant.

As the son approached his home, his father saw him from a distance and was filled with compassion. He ran to his son, embraced him, and kissed him. The son confessed his unworthiness, but the father called for the best robe, a ring, and sandals for his son. He also ordered a feast to celebrate his son's return, declaring, "This son of mine was dead and is alive again; he was lost and is found."

Meanwhile, the older son was working in the field. As he approached the house, he heard music and dancing. When he learned that the celebration was for his brother's return, he became angry and refused to join the feast. The father pleaded with him, but the older son complained that he had always been faithful, yet his father had never thrown a party for him. The father reassured the older son, saying, "You are always with me, and everything I have is yours. But we had to celebrate and be glad because this brother of yours was dead and is alive again; he was lost and is found." (Luke Chapter 15)

THE PARABLE OF the prodigal son is a beautiful illustration of God's unconditional love for us. As teenagers, you may face moments where you feel unworthy of love, whether because of mistakes you've made, failures you've experienced, or the weight of others' expectations. You may wonder if God could still love you after all you've done, or if you have to earn His love through good behavior.

But the father's response to the prodigal son shows us that God's love is not based on our performance or worthiness. The father didn't wait for his son to clean himself up or prove his repentance before embracing him. He ran to meet his son while he was still far off, showering him with love and restoration.

In the same way, God's love for you is unconditional and unshakable. No matter how far you may wander or how many times you stumble, God is always ready to welcome you back with open arms. His love is not earned by your achievements or lost by your failures. It is a constant, unchanging reality that flows from His very nature.

Moreover, the parable reminds us that God's love extends to all His children, even when we struggle to love each other. The older son's resentment and refusal to celebrate his brother's return reflects our own tendency to judge others or feel entitled to God's favor. But the father's pleading with the older son demonstrates God's heart for reconciliation and His desire for us to share in His love for one another.

As you navigate the ups and downs of teenage life, remember that you are deeply loved by a Heavenly Father who sees you, knows you, and loves you unconditionally. When you feel unworthy or distant from God, run into His open arms, trusting in His unwavering love and grace.

Reflection

• *In what moments or situations do you find it hardest to believe in or experience God's unconditional love?*

• *How can you embrace your identity as a beloved child of God, even when you face failure, rejection, or disappointment?*

• *In what ways can you extend God's unconditional love to others, especially those who may seem unlovable or undeserving?*

Prayer

Heavenly Father, thank You for Your unconditional love. Help us always return to You, knowing Your love is constant. Remind us that Your love is based on Your character, not our performance. Give us grace to extend Your love to others and find our security and joy in You. Amen.

2 7

THE TEN LEPERS

___ / ___ / _____

"Give thanks in all circumstances; for this is God's will for
you in Christ Jesus."

— 1 THESSALONIANS 5:18

*a*s Jesus was traveling to Jerusalem, he passed between the
regions of Samaria and Galilee. While entering a village, he
encountered a group of ten lepers standing at a distance. Due to the
severity of their condition and the customs of the time, they kept
their distance but cried out loudly, "Jesus, Master, have mercy on us."
Recognizing their plea, Jesus compassionately looked at them and
instructed, "Go and show yourselves to the priests."

In faith, the ten lepers obeyed and began their journey to the priests.
Remarkably, as they were on their way, they were cleansed of their
leprosy. Their skin, once ravaged by disease, became healthy and
whole. However, only one of the ten, upon realizing he had been
healed, was overwhelmed with gratitude. This man, a Samaritan,
turned back and returned to Jesus, shouting praises to God with a

loud and joyful voice. Overcome with thankfulness, he threw himself at Jesus' feet and gave thanks.

Jesus, noting the return of this single grateful man, asked, "Were not ten cleansed? Where are the other nine? Was no one found to return and give praise to God except this foreigner?" Acknowledging the man's faith and gratitude, Jesus said to him, "Rise and go your way; your faith has made you well." (Luke Chapter 17)

THE STORY of the ten lepers teaches us the importance of cultivating a heart of gratitude, even in the midst of life's challenges and blessings. As teenagers, it's easy to get caught up in the busyness and distractions of daily life, focusing on what we lack rather than what we have. We may take for granted the gifts, opportunities, and relationships God has given us, or become discontent when things don't go our way.

But the leper who returned to thank Jesus shows us the transformative power of gratitude. He recognized the incredible gift of healing he had received and took the time to express his thankfulness to Jesus. His gratitude set him apart from the other nine lepers who, though also healed, failed to return and give praise to God.

Gratitude is more than just a feeling; it's a choice and a practice that shapes our perspective and our lives. When we intentionally look for reasons to be thankful, even in difficult circumstances, we open our hearts to see God's goodness and provision. We shift our focus from what we don't have to what we do have, and we cultivate a spirit of contentment and joy.

Moreover, expressing gratitude to God and others deepens our relationships and points others to the source of our thankfulness. When we take the time to say "thank you," whether to a friend who has supported us, a teacher who has invested in us, or a parent who has sacrificed for us, we acknowledge their impact on our lives and reflect the love and generosity of Christ.

As you navigate the ups and downs of teenage life, make gratitude a daily habit. Start each day by thanking God for His blessings and provision, and look for opportunities to express appreciation to the people in your life. When you face challenges or disappointments, choose to find reasons to be grateful, trusting that God is at work in and through every circumstance.

Reflection

• *What are some specific blessings, gifts, or relationships in your life that you can thank God for today?*

• *In what situations or relationships do you struggle to express gratitude? How can you challenge yourself to cultivate a more thankful heart?*

• *How can your practice of gratitude be a witness to others and point them to the goodness and generosity of God?*

Prayer

Heavenly Father, thank You for Your countless blessings. Forgive us for taking Your goodness for granted. Help us cultivate thankfulness, even during challenges, and point others to You through our words and actions. May our lives overflow with gratitude and praise for who You are and all You have done. In Jesus' name, Amen.

28

MARTHA AND MARY

___ / ___ / _____

"My dear brothers and sisters, take note of this: Everyone should be quick to listen, slow to speak and slow to become angry."

— JAMES 1:19

*A*s Jesus and his disciples were traveling, they came to a village where two sisters, Martha and Mary, welcomed them into their home. Martha was busy preparing and serving the meal, while Mary sat at Jesus' feet, listening intently to his teachings. Frustrated, Martha complained to Jesus, asking him to tell Mary to help her. Jesus gently responded, "Martha, Martha, you are worried and upset about many things, but few things are needed—or indeed only one. Mary has chosen what is better, and it will not be taken away from her" (Luke Chapter 10).

As teens, it's easy to get caught up in the busyness of life, just like Martha. We have school, extracurricular activities, friends, and family demanding our attention. However, this story reminds us that amidst all the chaos, it's crucial to take time to sit at Jesus' feet and listen to his teachings, just as Mary did.

When we prioritize our relationship with God and actively listen to his word, we gain wisdom, peace, and guidance for navigating the challenges of life. By being good listeners, we open our hearts to God's voice and allow him to shape our character, strengthen our faith, and guide our decisions.

For example, when faced with peer pressure or difficult choices, listening to God's word can provide clarity and help us make decisions that align with our faith. By seeking God's guidance through prayer and Scripture, we can build stronger relationships, overcome obstacles, and grow in our personal and spiritual lives.

Reflection

• *In what areas of your life do you find yourself being more like Martha, busy and distracted? How can you intentionally create space to listen to God's voice?*

• *Think about a time when you faced a challenge or decision. How did listening to God's word or seeking godly advice help you navigate that situation?*

• *What practical steps can you take to cultivate a heart that listens to God and prioritizes your relationship with him?*

Prayer

Dear God, thank you for the wisdom and guidance found in the story of Martha and Mary. Help me to prioritize my relationship with you and to be a good listener, always seeking your voice amidst the busyness of life. Give me the strength to apply these lessons to my daily life. Amen.

THE PARABLE OF THE PHARISEE AND THE TAX COLLECTOR.

___ / ___ / _____

"When pride comes, then comes disgrace, but with humility comes wisdom."

— PROVERBS 11:2

*J*esus told this parable to some who trusted in themselves that they were righteous and treated others with contempt:

Two men went up into the temple to pray, one a Pharisee and the other a tax collector. The Pharisee, standing by himself, prayed: "God, I thank you that I am not like other men, extortioners, unjust, adulterers, or even like this tax collector. I fast twice a week; I give tithes of all that I get."

But the tax collector, standing far off, would not even lift up his eyes to heaven, but beat his breast, saying, "God, be merciful to me, a sinner!"

Jesus said, "I tell you, this man went down to his house justified, rather than the other. For everyone who exalts himself will be humbled, but the one who humbles himself will be exalted." (Luke Chapter 18)

IT'S SO easy to fall into the trap of comparing ourselves to others and feeling either superior or inferior - especially with the rise of social media. We may take pride in our accomplishments, appearance, or social status, or we may feel ashamed of our mistakes and shortcomings. However, the parable of the Pharisee and the Tax Collector reminds us that true righteousness comes from a humble spirit, not from our own merits.

When we approach God with humility, acknowledging our need for his mercy and grace, we open ourselves to a deeper relationship with him. By recognizing that we are all sinners in need of salvation, we can let go of the pride and self-righteousness that hinder our spiritual growth.

For example, if you find yourself judging others or feeling superior because of your talents or achievements, take a moment to reflect on the tax collector's prayer. Remind yourself that we are all equal in God's eyes and that our worth comes from his love, not our own abilities. By cultivating a humble spirit, you can build stronger, more compassionate relationships with others and draw closer to God.

Reflection

• *In what areas of your life do you struggle with pride or feelings of superiority? How can you practice humility in these situations?*

• *Think about a time when you felt ashamed or unworthy. How does the tax collector's prayer and Jesus' message of grace and mercy speak to those feelings?*

• *What practical steps can you take to cultivate a humble spirit in your daily life? How can you encourage and support others in their own journey towards humility?*

Prayer

Dear God, thank you for the powerful message of humility found in the parable of the Pharisee and the Tax Collector. Help me to let go of pride and self-righteousness, and to approach you with a humble and contrite heart. May I always remember that my worth comes from your love and grace. Amen.

30

THE PERSISTENT WIDOW

___ / ___ / _____

"Consider it pure joy, my brothers and sisters, whenever
you face trials of many kinds, because you know that
the testing of your faith produces perseverance."

— JAMES 1:2-3

*J*esus told his disciples a parable to show them that they should always pray and not give up. He said, "In a certain town, there was a judge who neither feared God nor cared about people. And there was a widow in that town who kept coming to him with the plea, 'Grant me justice against my adversary.'"

For some time, the judge refused. But finally, he said to himself, "Even though I don't fear God or care about people, yet because this widow keeps bothering me, I will see that she gets justice, so that she won't eventually come and attack me!"

And the Lord said, "Listen to what the unjust judge says. And will not God bring about justice for his chosen ones, who cry out to him day and night? Will he keep putting them off? I tell you, he will see that they get justice, and quickly. However, when the Son of Man comes, will he find faith on the earth?" (Luke Chapter 18)

THE PARABLE OF the persistent widow teaches us the value of patience and perseverance, especially in our prayer lives and faith journeys. As teenagers, you may face situations that seem unfair, overwhelming, or unresolved. You may pray for something for a long time without seeing any change, or face challenges that test your faith and resilience. In those moments, it's easy to become discouraged or give up hope.

But the widow in Jesus' parable shows us the power of persistent faith. Despite the judge's initial reluctance and the odds stacked against her, she refused to give up. She kept coming back, advocating for herself and believing that justice would be served. Her perseverance ultimately paid off, and the judge granted her request.

In the same way, God calls us to approach Him with persistent faith, even when we don't see immediate answers or resolutions. This doesn't mean that God is reluctant to help us or that we have to convince Him to act on our behalf. Rather, it means trusting in His wisdom, timing, and goodness, even when circumstances are difficult or confusing.

Patience and perseverance are essential qualities for navigating the challenges and uncertainties of teenage life. They enable us to keep going when we face setbacks, to trust God's plan even when it's unclear, and to develop the character and resilience needed to thrive in faith and life.

Moreover, the parable reminds us that God is a loving and just Father who hears our prayers and is committed to bringing about His purposes in our lives. When we cry out to Him day and night, He is moved by our faith and works on our behalf, even when we can't see it. As you face the ups and downs of teenage life, keep bringing your requests, fears, and hopes to God, trusting that He is at work and will bring about His best for you in His perfect timing.

Reflection

• *In what situations or areas of your life do you need to exercise patience and perseverance? How can you lean on God's strength and wisdom in those moments?*

• *What prayers or desires have you been bringing to God for a long time? How can you trust in His timing and goodness, even when you don't see immediate answers?*

• *How can your example of persistent faith and patient endurance be a witness to others and point them to the character of God?*

Prayer

Heavenly Father, thank You for the persistent widow's example. Help us trust You in challenges, rely on Your strength, and bring our requests to You. May our lives reflect Your goodness. In Jesus' name, Amen.

31

ZACCHAEUS THE TAX COLLECTOR

___ / ___ / _____

"Do not repay evil with evil or insult with insult. On the contrary, repay evil with blessing, because to this you were called so that you may inherit a blessing."

— 1 PETER 3:9

Zacchaeus, a wealthy chief tax collector in Jericho, was eager to see Jesus as He passed through the town. Due to his short stature and the large crowd, Zacchaeus ran ahead and climbed a sycamore tree to get a better view. To everyone's astonishment, when Jesus reached the spot, He looked up and called out to Zacchaeus, saying He would stay at his house that day.

This caused a stir among the crowd, who murmured in disapproval, knowing Zacchaeus was a notorious sinner. Despite the public's disdain, Zacchaeus joyfully welcomed Jesus into his home. Moved by Jesus' acceptance and love, Zacchaeus stood up and declared his repentance, promising to give half of his wealth to the poor and repay anyone he had cheated four times the amount.

Jesus, acknowledging Zacchaeus' sincere repentance, proclaimed, "Today salvation has come to this house, because this man, too, is a son of Abraham." This declaration affirmed Zacchaeus' transformation and inclusion among God's people (Luke 19:1-10).

As TEENS, you may encounter people who are difficult to love or get along with, such as classmates, teammates, or even family members. They may have different opinions, backgrounds, or habits that clash with your own. However, the story of Jesus and Zacchaeus reminds us that everyone, regardless of their past or reputation, is worthy of love and compassion.

By reaching out to those who are often overlooked or rejected, we follow Jesus' example and demonstrate the transformative power of love. When we show kindness and understanding to difficult people, we create opportunities for growth, healing, and redemption in their lives and our own.

For instance, if you have a classmate who often seems lonely or lashes out at others, you can choose to extend friendship and compassion. By inviting them to sit with you at lunch or partnering with them on a project, you may discover the reasons behind their behavior and help them experience the love of Christ through your actions.

Reflection

• *Think about someone in your life who you find difficult to love or get along with. How can you show them compassion and understanding, even when it's challenging?*

• *Reflect on a time when someone showed you love and acceptance, despite your flaws or mistakes. How did that experience impact you, and how can you extend that same grace to others?*

• *In what ways can you actively look for opportunities to reach out to those who may be overlooked or rejected in your school, community, or church?*

Prayer

Dear God, thank you for the example of Jesus and his love for Zacchaeus. Help me to see others through your eyes and to extend compassion and kindness to those who are difficult to love. Give me the courage to reach out and be a light in their lives. Amen.

32

THE WOMAN CAUGHT IN ADULTERY

___ / ___ / _____

"For we are God's handiwork, created in Christ Jesus to do
good works, which God prepared in advance for us
to do."

— EPHESIANS 2:10

One day, while Jesus was teaching in the temple courts, the teachers of the law and the Pharisees brought in a woman caught in adultery. They made her stand before the group and said to Jesus, "Teacher, this woman was caught in the act of adultery. In the Law, Moses commanded us to stone such women. Now what do you say?" They were using this question as a trap, in order to have a basis for accusing Jesus.

But Jesus bent down and started to write on the ground with his finger. When they kept on questioning him, he straightened up and said to them, "Let any one of you who is without sin be the first to throw a stone at her." Again he stooped down and wrote on the ground.

At this, those who heard began to go away one at a time, the older ones first, until only Jesus was left, with the woman still standing there. Jesus straightened up and asked her, "Woman, where are they? Has no one condemned you?"

"No one, sir," she said.

"Then neither do I condemn you," Jesus declared. "Go now and leave your life of sin." (John Chapter 8)

THE STORY of the woman caught in adultery teaches us the importance of self-respect and the power of Jesus' unconditional love and forgiveness. As teenagers, you may face situations where you feel ashamed, judged, or unworthy due to past mistakes, failures, or the opinions of others. In a world that often promotes a culture of shame and condemnation, it's easy to internalize negative messages and lose sight of your inherent worth and value.

But Jesus' response to the woman caught in adultery shows us a different way. When the religious leaders brought the woman before Him, ready to condemn and stone her, Jesus didn't join in their judgment. Instead, He challenged them to examine their own hearts and to recognize that we all fall short of God's perfect standard.

Jesus' words and actions demonstrate that our worth and dignity come not from our performance or the approval of others, but from the fact that we are beloved children of God. When Jesus refused to condemn the woman and instead offered her forgiveness and a fresh start, He was affirming her value and potential, despite her past mistakes.

As you navigate the challenges and pressures of teenage life, remember that your self-respect and identity are rooted in Christ's love for you. When you feel tempted to define yourself by your failures, your appearance, or the opinions of others, anchor your worth in the truth of who God says you are: chosen, beloved, and created in His image.

Moreover, Jesus' call to the woman to "go now and leave your life of sin" reminds us that true self-respect involves taking responsibility for our actions and seeking to live in a way that honors God and reflects His character. This doesn't mean striving for perfection, but rather, it means humbly acknowledging our need for grace and allowing God's love to transform us from the inside out.

Reflection

• *In what situations or relationships do you struggle most with self-respect, and how can you begin to anchor your worth and identity in Christ's love for you?*

• *How can you extend the same grace and forgiveness to yourself and others that Jesus extended to the woman caught in adultery?*

• *What practical steps can you take to cultivate a lifestyle of self-respect, rooted in your identity as a beloved child of God?*

Prayer

Heavenly Father, thank You for the example of love and forgiveness in the story of the woman caught in adultery. Help us find our worth in You, not in others' opinions or our performance. Give us courage to extend grace and forgiveness to ourselves and others. May our lives be marked by self-respect, rooted in Christ. In Jesus' name, Amen.

33
THE RESURRECTION OF LAZARUS

___ / ___ / _____

"Finally, all of you, be like-minded, be sympathetic, love one another, be compassionate and humble."

— 1 PETER 3:8

*L*azarus, a close friend of Jesus, became seriously ill. His sisters, Mary and Martha, sent word to Jesus, saying, "Lord, the one you love is sick." However, Jesus stayed where he was for two more days before going to Bethany, where Lazarus and his sisters lived.

By the time Jesus arrived, Lazarus had been dead for four days. Martha went out to meet Jesus and said, "Lord, if you had been here, my brother would not have died." Jesus replied, "Your brother will rise again." Martha thought He was speaking of the resurrection on the last day, but Jesus declared, "I am the resurrection and the life. The one who believes in me will live, even though they die; and whoever lives by believing in me will never die."

When Mary came to Jesus, she fell at His feet, weeping. Jesus saw her weeping, and the Jews who had come along with her also weeping.

He was deeply moved in spirit and troubled. He asked where they had laid Lazarus, and they took Him to the tomb. There, Jesus wept.

Jesus then ordered the stone to be taken away from the tomb and called out in a loud voice, "Lazarus, come out!" The dead man came out, his hands and feet wrapped with strips of linen, and a cloth around his face. Jesus said to them, "Take off the grave clothes and let him go." (John Chapter 11)

THE STORY of Jesus resurrecting Lazarus teaches us the importance of showing empathy towards others, especially those who are grieving or experiencing pain. As teenagers, you may encounter situations where your friends or classmates are going through difficult times, such as the loss of a loved one, a breakup, or a personal struggle. In those moments, it can be tempting to avoid the discomfort of their pain or to offer quick fixes and clichéd responses.

But Jesus' response to Mary and Martha's grief shows us a different way. When He saw them weeping, He didn't try to minimize their pain or offer empty platitudes. Instead, He entered into their sorrow and wept with them. His tears were a powerful expression of His love and compassion, a tangible reminder that He understood and shared in their heartache.

Showing empathy towards others means being willing to step into their shoes and to feel with them, even when it's uncomfortable or inconvenient. It means listening with an open heart, validating their experiences, and offering a supportive presence, rather than trying to fix or solve their problems.

Moreover, Jesus' resurrection of Lazarus reminds us that He has the power to bring hope and healing, even in the darkest of circumstances. When we show empathy towards others and point them to Jesus, we become channels of His love and grace, offering a glimpse of the redemption and restoration that He alone can provide.

As you navigate the relationships and challenges of teenage life, look for opportunities to practice empathy and compassion. When a friend shares a struggle or a painful experience, resist the urge to offer quick advice or to change the subject. Instead, take the time to listen, to acknowledge their feelings, and to offer a supportive presence. Pray with them and for them, trusting that God can work through your empathy to bring comfort, healing, and hope.

Reflection

• *In what situations or relationships do you find it most challenging to show empathy, and how can you ask God for the grace and wisdom to respond with compassion?*

• *How can you cultivate a heart of empathy, learning to listen with an open heart and to validate others' experiences and feelings?*

• *In what ways can your empathy and compassion be a witness to others of Jesus' love and grace, pointing them to the hope and healing that He alone can provide?*

Prayer

Heavenly Father, thank You for Jesus' example of empathy and compassion with Mary and Martha. Help us follow His footsteps by entering others' pain and offering support. Give us grace to listen with open hearts and point others to Your hope and healing. May our lives reflect Your love through deep empathy and compassion. In Jesus' name, Amen.

34

JESUS WASHES THE DISCIPLES' FEET

___ / ___ / _____

"For all those who exalt themselves will be humbled, and those who humble themselves will be exalted."

— LUKE 14:11

*I*t was the evening before Jesus' crucifixion, and He was sharing a final meal with His disciples. During the supper, Jesus got up from the table, took off His outer garment, and wrapped a towel around His waist. He then poured water into a basin and began to wash the disciples' feet, drying them with the towel.

When Jesus came to Simon, Peter objected, saying, "Lord, are you going to wash my feet?" Jesus replied, "You do not realize now what I am doing, but later you will understand." Peter protested, "No, you shall never wash my feet." Jesus answered, "Unless I wash you, you have no part with me."

After washing their feet, Jesus put on His clothes and returned to the table. He asked them, "Do you understand what I have done for you? You call me 'Teacher' and 'Lord,' and rightly so, for that is what I am. Now that I, your Lord and Teacher, have washed your feet, you also should wash one another's feet. I have set you an example that you should do as I have done for you." (John Chapter 13)

THE STORY of Jesus washing His disciples' feet teaches us the importance of humility in our relationships and in our walk with God. As teenagers, you may face pressure to assert your independence, prove your worth, or compete for status and recognition. In a world that often celebrates self-promotion and pride, Jesus' example of humility stands in stark contrast.

By washing His disciples' feet, a task typically reserved for the lowliest of servants, Jesus demonstrated that true greatness lies in serving others. He, the Son of God and the King of kings, humbled Himself and took on the role of a servant, showing us that no act of service is beneath us when it is done in love and obedience to God.

Moreover, Jesus' act of humility was not just a one-time event, but an example for us to follow. He instructed His disciples to wash one another's feet, symbolizing the importance of serving and caring for each other in the body of Christ. As you navigate the challenges and opportunities of teenage life, look for ways to practice humility by putting others' needs before your own, offering help and support, and being willing to do the unglamorous work of service.

Humility is not about thinking less of yourself, but about thinking of yourself less. It's about recognizing that your worth and identity come from God, not from your accomplishments, appearance, or status. When you embrace humility, you free yourself from the pressure to prove yourself and can instead focus on loving God and loving others.

Remember, Jesus, the ultimate example of humility, "did not consider equality with God something to be used to his own advantage; rather, he made himself nothing by taking the very nature of a servant"

(Philippians 2:6-7). As you seek to follow Jesus and grow in your faith, ask Him to cultivate a heart of humility within you, so that you may serve others with love and reflect His character to the world around you.

Reflection

• *In what areas of your life do you struggle with pride or the desire for recognition? How can you practice humility in those situations?*

• *What are some practical ways you can serve others and put their needs before your own, both in your daily life and in your faith community?*

• *How can your example of humility be a witness to others and point them to the servant heart of Jesus?*

Prayer

Heavenly Father, thank You for Jesus' example of humility in washing His disciples' feet. Help us serve others with love and put their needs before our own. Give us the strength to lay aside pride and seek our worth in You. May our lives reflect Your heart with a spirit of humility. In Jesus' name, Amen.

35

ANANIAS AND SAPPHIRA

___ / ___ / _____

"Whoever walks in integrity walks securely, but he who
makes his ways crooked will be found out."

— PROVERBS 10:9

*I*n the early days of the church, believers were sharing their possessions and giving to those in need. A man named Ananias, together with his wife Sapphira, sold a piece of property. However, they kept back part of the money for themselves and brought only a portion of it to lay at the apostles' feet, presenting it as the full amount.

Peter, filled with the Holy Spirit, confronted Ananias, saying, "Why has Satan filled your heart to lie to the Holy Spirit and keep back part of the price of the land? While it remained unsold, wasn't it your own? And after it was sold, wasn't the money at your disposal? Why have you conceived this deed in your heart? You haven't lied to men, but to God." Upon hearing these words, Ananias fell down and died. Great fear came upon all who heard about it. The young men came in, wrapped up his body, carried him out, and buried him.

About three hours later, Sapphira came in, unaware of what had happened. Peter asked her if they had sold the land for the price they had presented. She confirmed the amount, and Peter said, "How could you agree to test the Spirit of the Lord? Look, the feet of those who have buried your husband are at the door, and they will carry you out." Immediately, Sapphira fell down at Peter's feet and died. The young men came in, found her dead, and buried her beside her husband. Great fear came upon the whole church and all who heard about these events. (Acts Chapter 5)

THE STORY of Ananias and Sapphira is a stark reminder of the importance of honesty and integrity in our lives. As teenagers, you face numerous temptations and pressures to compromise your values, whether it's cheating on a test, lying to your parents, or pretending to be someone you're not on social media. It's easy to justify small acts of dishonesty, thinking that they don't matter or that no one will find out.

But Ananias and Sapphira's story shows us that God takes honesty and integrity seriously. Their sin was not in keeping back part of the money, but in lying about it and pretending to be more generous than they were. They were more concerned with their reputation and image than with being truthful before God and others.

As followers of Christ, we are called to live lives of authenticity and transparency, even when it's difficult or uncomfortable. This means being honest about our struggles, admitting our mistakes, and seeking forgiveness when we fall short. It means resisting the temptation to lie, cheat, or deceive, even in small ways, and choosing to honor God with our words and actions.

Moreover, the story of Ananias and Sapphira reminds us that our choices have consequences, not only for ourselves but for those around us. Their dishonesty brought judgment and death, and it struck fear in the hearts of all who heard about it. As you navigate the challenges of teenage life, remember that your decisions and actions have an impact on others, and strive to be a positive influence and example of integrity.

Reflection

• *In what areas of your life do you find it most challenging to be honest and live with integrity? How can you ask God for strength and courage to choose truth over deception?*

• *How can you cultivate a heart of authenticity and transparency in your relationships with God and others, even when it means admitting your struggles or mistakes?*

• *In what ways can your commitment to honesty and integrity be a witness to others and demonstrate the character of Christ?*

Prayer

Heavenly Father, thank You for reminding us of the importance of honesty and integrity. Help us resist lying or deceit and give us courage to live authentically. May our words and actions honor You and positively influence others. Grant us grace to admit mistakes, seek forgiveness, and grow in character. In Jesus' name, Amen.

36

THE JOURNEYS OF PAUL AND BARNABAS

___ / ___ / _____

"But encourage one another daily, as long as it is called 'Today,' so that none of you may be hardened by sin's deceitfulness."

— HEBREWS 3:13

*A*fter his conversion, Paul (formerly Saul) tried to join the disciples in Jerusalem, but they were afraid of him. Barnabas, however, brought Paul to the apostles and vouched for his genuine conversion. Later, when the church in Antioch grew, Barnabas was sent to encourage them. He then went to Tarsus to find Paul and bring him to Antioch, where they taught the believers for a year.

The Holy Spirit called Barnabas and Paul to go on a missionary journey. They traveled to Cyprus and then to cities in Asia Minor, preaching the gospel and establishing churches. In Lystra, the people tried to worship them as gods after Paul healed a lame man, but they rejected this and pointed the people to the true God.

On their return to Antioch, Barnabas and Paul reported all that God had done through them. However, a dispute arose concerning whether Gentile converts needed to follow Jewish laws. Barnabas and Paul, along with others, were sent to Jerusalem to discuss this issue with the apostles and elders. The council affirmed that Gentiles did not need to follow Jewish customs to be saved.

When planning their next missionary journey, Paul and Barnabas had a sharp disagreement about taking John Mark, who had previously left them. They parted ways, with Barnabas taking Mark and Paul choosing Silas. Despite this division, both teams continued to spread the gospel and strengthen the churches. (Acts Chapters 9 to 15)

THE STORY of Barnabas and Paul teaches us the transformative power of encouragement in our relationships and faith journeys. As teenagers, you have the opportunity to be a source of encouragement to those around you, whether it's a friend who is struggling, a classmate who is new to your school, or a younger sibling who looks up to you.

Encouragement is more than just offering compliments or positive words; it's about seeing the potential in others, advocating for them, and supporting them in their growth and development. Just as Barnabas recognized Paul's gifts and stood by him when others were doubtful, you can be the one who notices and affirms the strengths and abilities in others, even when they may not see it themselves.

Moreover, encouragement is a powerful tool for building up the body of Christ and advancing the gospel. When we encourage and support one another in our faith, we create a community of love, unity, and purpose. We spur one another on to deeper relationship with God and greater effectiveness in His mission.

As you navigate the challenges and opportunities of teenage life, look for ways to be a Barnabas to those around you. Offer words of affirmation and support, especially to those who may feel overlooked or discouraged. Stand up for others when they face skepticism or opposition, and be willing to vouch for their character and potential. Invest in relationships of mentorship and discipleship, both as a mentor and a mentee, recognizing the value of learning from and pouring into others.

Remember, your words and actions of encouragement have the power to shape lives and advance God's kingdom in ways you may never fully see or understand. Trust that as you obey God's call to encourage and build up others, He will use you to make an eternal impact and bring glory to His name.

Reflection

• *Who are the people in your life who need encouragement right now? How can you practically support and affirm them in their struggles or growth?*

• *In what ways have you experienced the impact of encouragement in your own life? How can you pay it forward and be a source of encouragement to others?*

• *How can your commitment to encouragement and building up others be a witness to the love and unity of Christ in your relationships and community?*

Prayer

Heavenly Father, thank You for Barnabas' example of encouragement. Help us see potential in others, support their growth, and build up the body of Christ. May our words and actions advance Your kingdom and reflect a spirit of encouragement and unity. In Jesus' name, Amen.

37

THE CONVERSION OF CORNELIUS

___ / ___ / _____

"There is neither Jew nor Gentile, neither slave nor free, nor is there male and female, for you are all one in Christ Jesus."

— GALATIANS 3:28

*C*ornelius, a centurion in the Italian Cohort, was a devout man who feared God and prayed continually. One day, he had a vision in which an angel told him to send for Peter, who was staying in Joppa.

Meanwhile, Peter went up on the housetop to pray and fell into a trance. He saw a vision of a great sheet descending from heaven, filled with all kinds of animals. A voice told him, "Rise, Peter; kill and eat." But Peter objected, saying he had never eaten anything common or unclean. The voice replied, "What God has made clean, do not call common." This happened three times before the sheet was taken back to heaven.

While Peter was pondering the vision, the men sent by Cornelius arrived. The Spirit told Peter to go with them, doubting nothing.

Peter went to Caesarea and entered Cornelius' house, where many people had gathered. Peter acknowledged that it was unlawful for a Jew to associate with or visit anyone of another nation, but God had shown him not to call any person common or unclean.

Cornelius shared his vision, and Peter began to speak, realizing that God shows no partiality and accepts those from every nation who fear Him and do what is right. As Peter spoke about Jesus, the Holy Spirit fell upon all who heard the message. The Jewish believers were amazed that the gift of the Holy Spirit had been poured out even on the Gentiles. Peter ordered that they be baptized in the name of Jesus Christ. (Acts Chapter 10)

As TEENS, you live in a diverse world filled with people from various cultures, races, and backgrounds. It's important to recognize that God's love extends to all people and that we are called to show respect and compassion to everyone, just as Peter learned through his encounter with Cornelius.

When we take the time to learn about and appreciate the unique customs, traditions, and perspectives of others, we enrich our own lives and build bridges of understanding. By treating people from different cultures with respect and kindness, we demonstrate the inclusive and transformative love of Christ.

For example, if you have classmates or friends from different cultural backgrounds, make an effort to learn about their traditions and experiences. Show interest in their stories and perspectives, and be open to expanding your own worldview. When you encounter someone who is different from you, remember that they are created and loved by God, just as you are.

Reflection

• *Have you ever experienced or witnessed discrimination or disrespect based on someone's cultural background? How did it make you feel, and what can you do to promote greater understanding and respect?*

• *Think about your own cultural background and experiences. How can you share your unique perspective with others while also being open to learning from them?*

• *In what ways can you actively seek out opportunities to build relationships with people from different cultures, both within your community and beyond?*

Prayer

Dear God, thank you for the example of Peter and Cornelius, which teaches us the importance of showing respect for all people, regardless of their cultural background. Help me to see others through your eyes and to extend your love and compassion to everyone I meet. May I be an instrument of your peace and understanding in this diverse world. Amen.

38

THE PHILIPPIAN JAILER'S
SALVATION

___ / ___ / _____

"I can do all this through him who gives me strength."

— PHILIPPIANS 4:13

*P*aul and Silas were traveling and preaching the gospel when they encountered a slave girl possessed by a spirit that enabled her to predict the future. For many days, she followed them, shouting, "These men are servants of the Most High God, who are telling you the way to be saved." Paul, troubled by her actions, cast out the spirit in the name of Jesus.

The girl's owners, realizing they had lost their source of income, seized Paul and Silas and dragged them before the authorities. The crowd joined in the attack, and the magistrates ordered them to be stripped and beaten with rods. After inflicting many blows, they threw Paul and Silas into prison, ordering the jailer to guard them securely.

Despite their painful circumstances, Paul and Silas chose to maintain a positive attitude. Around midnight, they were praying and singing hymns to God, and the other prisoners were listening to them.

Suddenly, a violent earthquake shook the prison, and all the doors flew open, and everyone's chains came loose.

The jailer, assuming the prisoners had escaped, drew his sword to kill himself. But Paul shouted, "Don't harm yourself! We are all here!" The jailer called for lights, rushed in, and fell trembling before Paul and Silas. He then brought them out and asked, "Sirs, what must I do to be saved?" They replied, "Believe in the Lord Jesus, and you will be saved—you and your household." The jailer and his entire family came to faith in Christ that very night. (Acts Chapter 16)

THE STORY of Paul and Silas in prison teaches us the transformative power of a positive attitude, even in the face of adversity. As teenagers, you may encounter situations that feel unfair, painful, or overwhelming. Maybe you're facing bullying, family conflicts, academic stress, or personal struggles. In those moments, it's easy to give in to negativity, self-pity, or despair.

But Paul and Silas' example shows us that we have a choice in how we respond to difficult circumstances. Instead of complaining or becoming bitter, they chose to pray and praise God, even in the darkness of their prison cell. Their positive attitude not only sustained them through their trial but also had a profound impact on those around them.

The other prisoners were listening to Paul and Silas' prayers and hymns, witnessing the joy and peace they had in Christ, despite their suffering. When the earthquake struck and the doors flew open, Paul and Silas' concern for the jailer's well-being demonstrated the depth of their faith and the genuineness of their message. Their positive attitude paved the way for the jailer and his family to come to salvation.

As you face the challenges and pressures of teenage life, remember that your attitude is a powerful witness to others. When you choose to maintain a positive outlook, rooted in your faith in Christ, you reflect the hope and resilience that comes from knowing Him. Your example can be a light in the darkness, pointing others to the source of your strength and joy.

Moreover, a positive attitude is not about denying or ignoring the reality of your struggles, but about choosing to trust in God's goodness and sovereignty, even when life is hard. It's about fixing your eyes on Jesus, the author and perfecter of your faith, and allowing His perspective to shape your own.

Reflection

• *In what situations do you find it most challenging to maintain a positive attitude? How can you lean on God's strength and truth in those moments?*

• *How can your positive attitude and faith in Christ be a witness to others, especially those who are struggling or searching for hope?*

• *What are some practical ways you can cultivate a positive attitude, such as practicing gratitude, memorizing Scripture, or surrounding yourself with encouraging influences?*

Prayer

Heavenly Father, thank You for Paul and Silas' example of a positive attitude. Help us choose joy and faith in adversity, trusting in Your goodness. May our lives witness hope and resilience in Christ. Give us strength to fix our eyes on Jesus and let His perspective shape ours. In His name, Amen.

39

THE ROAD TO EMMAUS

___ / ___ / _____

"The LORD is close to the brokenhearted and saves those
who are crushed in spirit."

— PSALM 34:18

On the same day that Jesus rose from the dead, two of his disciples were walking to a village called Emmaus. As they talked about the events surrounding Jesus' death, Jesus himself came up and walked with them, but they were kept from recognizing him.

Jesus asked them what they were discussing, and they shared their sadness and confusion about Jesus' crucifixion and the reports of his resurrection. Jesus then explained to them, beginning with Moses and all the Prophets, how the Scriptures pointed to the Messiah and his suffering.

As they approached Emmaus, Jesus acted as if he were going farther, but the disciples urged him to stay with them. When he was at the table with them, he took bread, gave thanks, broke it, and began to give it to them. Then their eyes were opened, and they recognized him, but he disappeared from their sight.

The disciples said to each other, "Were not our hearts burning within us while he talked with us on the road and opened the Scriptures to us?" They immediately returned to Jerusalem and found the eleven disciples and others assembled, saying, "It is true! The Lord has risen and has appeared to Simon." Then the two told what had happened on the road and how Jesus was recognized by them when he broke the bread. (Luke Chapter 24)

THE STORY of the disciples on the road to Emmaus teaches us valuable lessons about dealing with disappointment in our faith journeys. As teenagers, you may face situations that leave you feeling disappointed, confused, or even hopeless. Maybe you've experienced a difficult breakup, a failed friendship, a poor academic performance, or a shattered dream. In those moments, it's easy to feel like God has abandoned you or that your faith has been misplaced.

But the disciples' experience reminds us that Jesus is always with us, even when we don't recognize His presence or understand His plan. Just as He walked alongside the disciples in their disappointment, He walks with us in our struggles, offering comfort, guidance, and hope.

Moreover, the story highlights the importance of turning to Scripture and biblical truth in times of disappointment. When the disciples were confused and disheartened, Jesus opened their eyes to the prophecies concerning the Messiah, showing them how God's plan was being fulfilled even in the midst of their pain. As you face disappointments and uncertainties, immerse yourself in God's Word, trusting that He will use it to speak truth, hope, and purpose into your life.

The disciples' journey also reminds us of the power of community in dealing with disappointment. When they recognized Jesus and experienced the joy of His resurrection, they immediately returned to share the good news with their fellow disciples. As you navigate the ups and downs of teenage life, surround yourself with a community of believers who can encourage you, pray for you, and point you back to Jesus when you're struggling.

Remember, disappointment is a natural part of life, but it doesn't have to define or defeat you. As you bring your disappointments to Jesus, trust that He is at work in and through them, shaping you into the person He created you to be and using your experiences to bring glory to His name.

Reflection

• *What are some of the disappointments or shattered hopes you're currently facing, and how can you invite Jesus into those struggles?*

• *How can you prioritize reading and studying Scripture, especially in times of disappointment or confusion?*

• *Who are the trusted friends, mentors, or community members you can turn to for support and encouragement when you're dealing with disappointment?*

Prayer

Heavenly Father, thank You for the disciples on the road to Emmaus, reminding us of Your constant presence. Help us seek Your Word and our faith community for guidance and strength, trusting Your plan even in confusion. May our disappointments become opportunities for growth and deeper faith. In Jesus' name, Amen.

40

PAUL'S LESSON ON
CONTENTMENT

___ / ___ / _____

*Keep your lives free from the love of money and be content
with what you have, because God has said, 'Never will
I leave you; never will I forsake you.'"*

— HEBREWS 13:5

*A*postle Paul, writing from prison, expresses his gratitude to
the Philippians for their concern and support. He acknowl-
edges that they have revived their care for him, though they had
lacked the opportunity to show it earlier. Paul then shares a profound
truth about contentment:

"I am not saying this because I am in need, for I have learned to be
content whatever the circumstances. I know what it is to be in need,
and I know what it is to have plenty. I have learned the secret of being
content in any and every situation, whether well fed or hungry,
whether living in plenty or in want. I can do all this through him who
gives me strength".

Paul had experienced both abundance and hardship in his life and
ministry. He had faced persecution, imprisonment, shipwrecks, and

countless trials. Yet, through it all, he had learned to find contentment in Christ, regardless of his external circumstances. (Philippians Chapter 4)

THE STORY of Apostle Paul's journey to contentment teaches us that true satisfaction and peace come not from our possessions, achievements, or circumstances, but from our relationship with Christ. As teenagers, you may face pressure to find contentment in temporary things like popularity, grades, relationships, or material possessions. The world often tells us that we need more, better, or different things to be happy and fulfilled.

But Paul's example shows us that contentment is a choice and a learned skill. It's about shifting our focus from what we lack to what we have in Christ. When we root our identity and satisfaction in Him, we can experience peace and joy, even in the midst of challenges and uncertainties.

Learning to be content doesn't mean that we never experience hardship or that we become complacent in our circumstances. Rather, it means that we trust in God's goodness and provision, even when life is difficult. It means finding our strength and sufficiency in Christ, who empowers us to face every situation with grace and resilience.

As you navigate the ups and downs of teenage life, cultivate a heart of gratitude and contentment. Instead of constantly comparing yourself to others or seeking fulfillment in temporary things, fix your eyes on Jesus and the eternal hope and security you have in Him. Practice thankfulness for the blessings in your life, no matter how small they may seem, and trust that God is working all things together for your good and His glory.

Remember, contentment is not a one-time achievement, but a daily choice to surrender your desires and trust in God's perfect plan for your life. As you learn to find your satisfaction in Christ, you'll discover a deep sense of peace, purpose, and joy that transcends your circumstances.

Reflection

• *In what areas of your life do you struggle most with contentment, and how can you begin to shift your focus to finding satisfaction in Christ?*

• *What practical steps can you take to cultivate a heart of gratitude and thankfulness, even in the midst of challenges or disappointments?*

• *How can your example of contentment in Christ be a witness to others and point them to the source of true satisfaction and peace?*

Prayer

Heavenly Father, thank You for Paul's example of contentment. Help us find satisfaction and peace in You, not in temporary things. Give us wisdom and strength to choose gratitude and trust, even in difficulties. May our lives witness the joy and contentment from knowing You. In Jesus' name, Amen.

KEEPING THE FAITH ALIVE

"Therefore encourage one another and build each other up,
just as in fact you are doing."

— 1 THESSALONIANS 5:11

*N*ow that you've completed "*10-Minute Bible Stories for Teens*," you have a wealth of knowledge and inspiration to help you navigate life's challenges and grow in your faith. It's time to pass on your newfound wisdom and show other young readers where they can find the same guidance.

Simply by leaving your honest opinion of this book on Amazon, you'll show other teenagers where they can find the encouragement and insights they're looking for, and help them discover the power of God's Word in their own lives.

Thank you for your help. The Christian faith is kept alive when we pass on our knowledge and share the love of God with others – and you're helping Biblical Teachings to do just that.

Scan below to leave your review on Amazon

SCAN ME

Your review is a testament to your journey of faith and a beacon of hope for other young believers. By sharing your thoughts, you're not only supporting the mission of Biblical Teachings but also fulfilling God's call to spread His message of love and truth.

Remember, your words have the power to change lives and lead others closer to Christ. So, take a moment to reflect on the impact these stories have had on your own spiritual growth, and consider how your review could be the very thing that inspires another teenager to embark on their own journey of faith.

Thank you for being a part of this community of young believers who are passionate about living out God's Word and making a difference in the world. May God continue to bless you and use you as a light in the lives of others.

With gratitude,

Biblical Teachings

AND SO, THE JOURNEY CONTINUES...

Congratulations, young reader! You've made it through "*10 Minute Bible Stories for Teens*" – a journey filled with timeless wisdom, powerful lessons, and relatable insights. I hope these stories have entertained you and inspired you to grow in your faith and apply God's truth to your daily life.

Remember, the lessons learned from these stories are not meant to stay within these pages. They are intended to be lived out in the real world as you face the challenges, joys, and uncertainties of being a teenager in the 21st century. Whether you're dealing with peer pressure, struggling with self-doubt, or searching for your purpose, know that *God's word is a lamp unto your feet and a light unto your path* (Psalm 119:105).

As you continue your faith journey, I encourage you to seek God's wisdom and guidance. Stay connected to Him through prayer, reading the Bible, and surrounding yourself with a supportive community of believers. And don't forget – your story is still being written. Trust that God has an amazing plan for your life, and have faith that He will guide you every step of the way.

Thank you for allowing us to be a part of your spiritual journey. It has been an honor and a privilege to share these stories with you. We pray they will continue to inspire, challenge, and draw you closer to God's heart. May you always remember that you are loved, valued, and destined for greatness in Christ.

Keep shining bright. The best is yet to come.

With love and prayers,

Biblical Teachings

P.S. Keep your eye out for Part 2 and, if you like, check out our other books on Amazon. There's always more to discover and learn on this exciting journey of faith!

Made in United States
North Haven, CT
14 July 2024

54792272R00085